DIAMOND AIR

THE WITCH BROTHERS SAGA, BOOK TWO

ADAM J. RIDLEY

BLAKE ALLWOOD PUBLISHING

Adam J. Ridley
Visit my website at adamjridley.com

Printed in the United States of America
Box Elder, SD

First Printing: August 2022
Blake Allwood Publishing
Ebook ISBN: 978-1-956727-30-2
Paperback ISBN: 978-1-956727-31-9
Library of Congress Control Number: 2022914084

CONTENT WARNINGS

Homophobia
Controlling Parents
Explicit Sex Scenes
Child Abuse
Violence

Join Blake's email list to get advance notice of new books and receive his occasional newsletter:

www.blakeallwood.com

MM Romance **By Blake Allwood**	**Romantic Fantasy** **By Adam J. Ridley**

MM Romance
By Blake Allwood

Transitions Series
Aiden Inspired
Suzie Empowered (MF Romance)
Bobby Transformed

Chance Series
Love By Chance
Another Chance With Love
Taking A Chance For Love

Romantic Series
Romantic Renovations (1)
Romantic Rescue (2)
Romantic Recon (3)

Melody Series
Melody of the Heart
Melody of the Snow

Road to Rocktoberfest Anthology
Changing His Tune - 2022

Coming Home Series (2023)
A Long Way Home
Family Home
Down Home
…and many more

Novellas
Tenacious
Moon's Place

Romantic Fantasy
By Adam J. Ridley

Big Bend Series
Love's Legacy (1)
Love's Heirloom (2)
Love's Bequest (3)

The Witch Brothers Series
Emerald Earth
Diamond Air
Ruby Fire
Sapphire Water

ACKNOWLEDGMENTS

Special thanks to the following amazing people who helped me get this book finished and into your hands.
Jo Bird: Editor
Renee Mizar: Editor
Alma Alexander: Editor
Ann Attwood: Proofreader

And of course, a big thank you to my husband who puts up with my endless stories and handles the formatting and final publishing of all my books.

ONE

PROLOGUE: THREE YEARS BEFORE

LANCE

RAGE SURGED THROUGH ME like a flooded river. When Tom, my husband, finally noticed me standing in the doorway, he pushed the man off and jumped up, saying, "You aren't supposed to be home yet." Like *that* was a perfectly reasonable explanation for walking in on your husband fucking another man in your bed.

The ugly man–though in truth, I saw more of his ass than his face–managed to escape as I hurled things around the bedroom. I grabbed whatever was within reach, not caring what among our possessions was broken or shattered.

As the rage settled and I slowly came back into myself, the room was in tatters, and Tom was gone. I was alone, standing among the ruins of my relationship. Three years of loss landed on me with a profound and deep pain.

Tears streaked down my cheeks as I sat on the bed. I kept asking myself what had gone wrong. I'd vetted Tom, refusing to let him get too close, until I was certain he was a good guy. Even though I'd talked to his friends, interviewing them, which at the time amused him, I still had somehow chosen the wrong man... again.

I must've sat on the end of that bed for hours, the bed we'd shared, the bed where I'd allowed myself to trust again. Even though I was afraid of trusting, even though I didn't really want to have my heart broken again, I'd stupidly allowed myself to trust Tom.

Depression settled in the moment Tom left, then got worse once the divorce was final. I took a leave from work, and began preparing myself for a life of solitude. There wouldn't be another Tom, I resolved. I just wouldn't... couldn't let myself go through that again.

My father had cursed me as a teenager to never knowing a man's love... I'd tried so hard to pretend that was just make-believe. It was getting harder to blow off as hocus pocus, though, when my string of broken relationships–Tom being the latest and most painful–proved otherwise.

If I was being honest, the depression was becoming less about a cheating asshole of a husband, and more about my dad's fucking curse winning. That said a lot... That said too much, really.

On the bright side, the demise of my marriage didn't hamper my professional life. If anything, with Tom now gone, I was able to give myself entirely over to work. I'd been a successful attorney, working in and out of the federal government since leaving grad-school. I'd worked closely with congressional leaders, senators, and even presidents on both sides of the political divide.

I'd also, had *some* success in my personal life. I'd moved to New York after law school, and became friends with a couple to whom I later agreed to be a sperm donor. We shared custodial responsibility for our daughter, Jennie, who was a shining light among the darkness, and there was *a lot* of darkness.

Bolstering myself after the divorce, I sold my part of the law firm, packed up my apartment, and moved back home to Oregon with my tail between my legs. My friend and former college roommate was the governor, and he convinced me to run for attorney general.

"You're a natural, and if you're going to be in Oregon anyway, why not join in on the fun?" Gerald asked.

"*Fun* my ass," I told him. "I've been in politics my entire career. It's a lot of crap on top of more crap, and seldom any fun."

He ended up nudging me into filing as a candidate, and I really didn't think I'd win, but apparently the voters had other ideas, because less than a year after moving back, I was elected as Oregon's next attorney general.

Riding high on my win didn't take away the lingering undercurrent of depression, though. My heart was jaded, and even though I'd been asked out by several men since taking office, I declined them all. Politics and dating didn't seem to work well. Also, my mind was tainted with visions of my ex being fucked by the ugly man, and no matter how I thought about it, it always sent the same message. *Men will always betray me, because I'm not someone who can be loved.*

With that message continually running in the background, how could I be anything other than single? I stared at the divorce papers, torturing myself by yet again reading through the last connection I had with the man who broke my heart, before tossing them into a file I had every intention of burying as deep as I could in my home office. *Dad, you absolute fucking asshole. You win!*

Two

Present Day

Lance

"Hey, brothers," I said, smiling at the computer screen showing my two younger siblings' faces smiling back at me. "Hey, once again, I'm sorry I couldn't get free to meet at Crater Lake. Things have just... well, they've gotten hectic." I felt guilty, because I was actually sort of lying. Yes, of course, I was busy but mostly, I didn't want to see them feeling sorry for me over the stupid divorce. I really should be over this shit by now, and didn't need to continue dragging them through it like I did to myself.

"Wait," Kyle said, as he turned to talk to someone in his office. "Really? They think it's gonna be soon?"

Kyle turned off his audio and walked away from the screen. Crea and I watched as he talked to someone in the background, before coming back a moment later, looking as if he was about to explode with excitement. "Sorry, guys—" he said after turning the audio back on, "—but I have to go. Popocatepetl looks as if it might blow. Let's try this again after I get back from Mexico."

We watched as he scrambled out of his chair and out the door, forgetting to shut off his Zoom.

"Well, that was very... Kyle," Crea said.

"Yep, well, I should probably go too."

"No, wait. I wanted to tell you I met someone, and more importantly, I'm moving back to Chemeketa."

My mouth fell open, shocked by what Crea was saying. The one thing we all agreed on was that none of us ever wanted to live in Chemeketa again. "What do you mean, moving back?"

He shrugged. "Already done, and you know the guy I met. Jennie said you're a big fan of Eli Bane. We're sorta engaged."

My first thought was, *Oh well, gonna lose that connection*, which was awful of me but also the truth. My daughter and I were both huge fans of the artist's work, even more so since she'd become his apprentice, but there was also no denying that my brothers sucked at relationships as much as I did. If Crea was with him now, Eli would likely hate us both when their relationship inevitably flopped.

"Yeah, that's good, buddy," I said, forcing myself to smile.

"God, you're shitty at hiding your emotions. How have you survived as an attorney?"

"Very well, thank you very much," I said, and Crea laughed.

"So, I need to talk to you about the curse..." The Zoom meeting began to break up then, and eventually showed a swirling circle at the bottom of my screen before a notice popped up saying the connection had been lost.

Saved by the... well, by the whatever screwed up the internet connection.

I quickly texted Crea.

Sorry, my internet went down, let's talk later. I wanna know more about you moving to Chemeketa.

I couldn't have really cared less, if I was being honest. As long as I didn't have to move there, all was good, and I was happy enough.

Although, I did need to go there to finalize my late grandmother's estate. I was sure her roommate would like that to be done, not that I gave a damn what he wanted. *The mooch.* Well, maybe that wasn't entirely accurate, but he was *something.*

Regardless, I was glad to be off the hook for now. No visiting brothers, no Zoom talk, and no reason to remember the hell that was my family.

Three

Drew

I SAT IN THE little clearing where all of Chemeketa had gathered to release Gwen's ashes. The day was blustery, like it tended to be on the Oregon coast this time of year, but the townsfolk had come together and magically pushed back the rain clouds, allowing the early fall sun to filter into the clearing long enough for us all to say goodbye.

Chemeketa was the sort of small town where everyone knew everyone, and I had little doubt Gwen held a special place in everyone's hearts. If the turnout for scattering her ashes was any indication, my former roommate had been well-respected and loved.

"Drew," Mayor Katan Manning said, drawing me out of my thoughts. "Would you like to say a few words?"

I nodded, then slowly made my way up to the front of the large crowd.

I didn't need notes to speak from my heart about the woman who, in many ways, had become the most important person in my life.

"Gwendolyn Franklyn saved me from my own miserable life," I said and let it hang there. "Most of you know bits and pieces of my life before I came to Chemeketa. I had very few people I trusted and even fewer people who knew about my... gifts. Gwen embraced me, and I mean that quite literally. She grabbed me and never let go."

Several people in the crowd chuckled, because Gwen was tenacious in every way possible.

"She was a grandmother, mentor, and friend... wonderfully quirky, vibrant, accepting, and loving. She was truly one of a kind, and will be missed on this side of the veil."

I didn't say a lot that day, partly because it was still so hard referring to Gwen in the past tense, and because I couldn't say much about her that everyone there didn't already know. Mostly, as I spoke, I just wanted to thank her, and thank her friends, for embracing me as freely as they had.

Soon after arriving in Chemeketa, Gwen had tried to convince me to join her coven, and honestly, I considered it, but it just wasn't really for me. Despite that, they'd all been a comfort to me since she died. Usually, they only met a couple times a year, because, when you lived in a magical community like Chemeketa, there wasn't much need for regular coven meetings, but they'd all surrounded me with Gwen's passing, and their support and friendships were another of the many things Gwen had gifted me.

I smiled as I sat in our living room, across from the fireplace like Gwen and I had done so many times before. I'd asked her once, early on in our friendship, what the nature of our relationship really was and she'd smiled, and said, "Well, I think for me you're like one of my grandsons."

That felt right then, and even more so over time. Gwen not only filled the void where *my* family should've been, but I thought I did the same for her, especially since Gwen's grandsons hardly ever came around.

I went to the liquor cabinet and pulled out the Bénédictine and Brandy we sipped only on the coldest of nights. The weather was mild, but I was feeling rather cold tonight. Well, more emptied out if I was honest. Even though we both knew it was coming, her transition had been torture for me. It seemed like she was here one moment, and gone the next.

Well, *mostly* gone. Since her death, she'd a tendency to show up at the oddest times, but I kept telling her to stop fussing and try to transition like a proper witch should. Did she listen? Of course not. The woman had never grasped the art of listening, never mind being told what to do.

Tonight, I didn't really feel my friend's spirit though, just me alone in the home we'd shared. I chuckled and sat back down with my drink and years of good memories. Gwen had asked me to move in with her the last few years of her life, when the property had become too much for her to manage alone. I'd been living in an apartment outside of Chemeketa on a farm owned by a fellow witch, and didn't hesitate moving in to help out. More than a few eyebrows went up at the news of us shacking up together. Despite the fact that she and I were just friends, and my being gay, we didn't do much to dispel the rumors... it was fun stirring the small-town rumor mill. Not that anyone in Chemeketa really cared what people got up to behind closed doors.

Townsfolk also liked to gossip about how Gwen's grandsons hardly ever visited. We'd flown up to Seattle, then down to San Francisco to visit Crea a few times over the years, but I had yet to meet the eldest Franklyn brother. Not that I was always home, since I traveled a lot for work, but as far as I knew, Lance hadn't set foot in Chemeketa since leaving for college. Thinking about that left a bad taste—*he must really be a callous asshole*—I knew how much Gwen loved and missed her grandsons, and never stopped singing their praises. No joke, the woman would talk about all three of them constantly, then laugh when I'd roll my eyes at yet another family story. Gods, I missed her.

Almost a full year after Gwen's death, her grandson Crea finally came to retrieve the items she'd left him. I helped him bring the chest from the attic and stored it in his car, and then made sure he had the little wooden box containing the ring she'd had made for him.

That night, I began having nightmares. Somehow I knew the dreams were associated with some unresolved issues surrounding her three grandsons, but I wasn't sure how or why. I just assumed once they had all picked up their heirlooms, the dreams would stop... at least, I hoped so.

I didn't have much time to focus on that, though, because with Gwen being gone, I had adopted many of her town duties, including preparing for the upcoming Lammas Festival. Lammas, that was the day to face your fears. Harvest was the foundation for the holiday, but not all harvests would bring in enough bounty to fill the cupboards. While it could bring celebration, it could also bring disaster.

I intentionally refused three singing gigs, because I wanted to be home for Lammas, much to the chagrin of my bandmates. Remaining in Chemeketa just felt important this year.

As we closed in on the August first holiday, the dreams began to intensify. They were always about the same thing—a man coming into my life, but it was unclear whether he was good luck, or if he brought about destruction. Some nights, I saw images of my... well, I wasn't sure what you'd call him. My potential lover? My destined mate?

No, not the last one. I believed we'd make our own destiny, which, yeah, wasn't very pious of me. I'd always struggled with rules and following dogma, even the Catholicism of my childhood. So, although I supported my Wiccan brothers and sisters, I personally avoided any organized religion, be it paganism or otherwise. I smiled to myself as I thought, if the deities wanted to put sexy men in my path, though, I'd be happy to play along.

Typically, my dreams offered glimpses and visions of possible outcomes, but I was never gifted in the art of divination. When I would dream of men, I'd never see anyone specific, just the general types I found attractive. This past week's dreams had all been enjoyable, some featuring a tall blond and others a stocky brunet... until they turned menacing.

The day after Lammas, I woke with a splitting headache. I'd left my window open during the night, and a cool breeze was dancing in and out of the room, blowing the curtains.

"Damn," I said as I sat up, and held my head in my hands.

I closed my eyes and drew in a deep breath, drawing energy from the breeze, and envisioning the cool air becoming warm. I held it deep in my lungs for a moment before breathing out, instantly feeling the warmth fill the room. It was a clever trick Gwen had taught me, although she wasn't very good at it since she wasn't an air elemental like me.

I drew in another breath, this time, letting myself taste the elements it contained. The salty sea air, smoke from a neighbor's fire, the smell of pines from the great forest...

As soon as that breath filled my lungs, I felt a cool, soothing energy flow through my chest and up to my skull, and the headache eased, but with it came a warning. *He's coming.*

Premonitions like that weren't uncommon for me. I'd had them all my life. Even as a kid, something would warn me whenever my father was on the warpath, but premonitions like this one, accompanied by a headache or pain of any kind, indicated I was somehow blocking the energy flow. It almost always meant something externally painful would be coming my way or rather, *someone*.

Of course, I didn't really need a premonition to know who was coming. Lance was the executor of his grandmother's estate, and he had yet to show up to settle it even though it had been over a year since her death. The man had rubbed me the wrong way for as long as I knew Gwen had a grandson named Lance. I couldn't really explain my instant dislike and irritation even at just hearing his name, but I couldn't shake it. It was just... a feeling.

Fortunately, for me and probably him, since I wasn't sure how I was going to act when I finally met him, there wasn't much of an estate to settle. Gwen had sold the house to me not long after I moved in with her. "You need to know the property is yours now," she'd said, like she had some kind of premonition about how her grandsons would deal with me.

The will had been cut and dried, so the only thing that had to be done was to distribute the few heirlooms mentioned in it.

I wasn't surprised it'd taken so long for her grandsons to show up. Gwen had seen it coming and told me they would need time to mourn before they could face her loss. She also hinted toward the fact that she was re-sponsible for keeping them away after she'd gotten sick. "I don't want the boys to remember me as a feeble old woman," she said one morning. Gwen was a prideful and powerful witch, so I had no doubt if she'd cast a spell to keep the men away, they'd have *definitely* stayed away. A childish part of me secretly hoped that Lance felt at least some guilt for never having visited beforehand... again, I couldn't fully explain my utter contempt for the man, but I felt it deep in my bones.

I crawled out of bed, got dressed, had coffee, and went into the living room to wait for the jackass. Having never met him in person, I still felt like I knew him based on

Gwen's stories, and what I'd heard about his high-profile political career, and from the locals who remembered him as a teenager. Despite Gwen heaping praise whenever she talked about her grandsons, I couldn't get past how Lance had essentially abandoned his grandmother upon turning eighteen. It was going to take all that was in me to remain civil around the man.

As predicted, Lance arrived with all the authority and arrogance befitting his title of state attorney general. For the most part, I wasn't intimidated by him. Of course, nothing I'd ever heard about Lance prepared me for how incredibly handsome he was.

The guy had to be every bit of six three, maybe six four. His shoulders were broad and tapered to a perfect V-shaped waist. I couldn't help wondering what it'd feel like to run my tongue over that V-shaped... *Fuck. No. This was what the warning was about. Leave Gwen's arrogant asshole of a selfish grandson alone.*

Of course, I was instantly suspicious of my attraction to Lance. This had my dearly departed roommate's meddlesome, spellcasting fingerprints all over it. Witches in her coven had as many diverse interests as the rest of the population, among them healers, horticulturalists, environmentalists, dabblers in politics, and those who enjoyed helping lost souls find their way through the veil. Gwen, as it happened, was a love-spell witch, never mind she'd already tried fixing me up with every available gay man this side of the Willamette Valley.

Gwen loved all things romantic, and her gardens, spells, and social life were all about that pursuit. While living with her, I quickly lost count of the number of people who showed up at our door asking her to cast some spell or other for love.

Her approach was more therapeutic than spellcasting, but she was good at it, no matter her methods. That also meant the witch wasn't above trying to push her grandson on me, even from across the veil.

The tension between us was high from the moment I answered the door. When Lance came into the house after giving me a curt nod rather than an actual greeting, I immediately handed him the small wooden box with his name scribbled on the bottom that Gwen had left sitting on the fireplace mantle in the living room. My back muscles began to tighten, making me feel like I needed a chiropractor, so I wasted no time in trying to move things along so that he and his things would be out of my home and life as quickly as possible.

Without waiting for him to open the box, I escorted him to the attic where Gwen had laid out three early twentieth-century turtleback chests, one for each grandson. Crea had already taken his, so now only two sat waiting to be collected.

I had no idea what was in them, and Gwen had instructed me not to be in the attic when the men opened them. I was to show them where they were, hand them the letter she'd written, and tell them the key to their box was in the envelope. I handed Lance his envelope and turned to leave.

"Don't you want to know what's in it?" he asked.

I shook my head. "Nope, Gwen was clear this was private, and I was to leave you each alone in the attic to go through the items she'd saved for you alone. I'll be in the living room when you're done. I can help you bring the chest downstairs when you're ready."

I went down to the living room and opened the book I'd just started reading when Lance had knocked on my door. Was it rude that he just showed up unannounced? I wasn't quite ready to decide yet, and the truth was, it didn't matter. I had something that belonged to him, and until it was taken, my promise to Gwen went unfulfilled. I assumed she wouldn't rest until all the items were distributed, and I was concerned about her spirit. It didn't do for the spirits to linger long between the two worlds. Too many variables could affect their path to the next chapter of existence.

"I was supposed to have a vial of my grandmother's... um, she called it her potion... in my chest," I heard him say as he came down the stairs, about an hour after I'd left him. "In her letter, she said it was important, but it wasn't with the other stuff. Do you know where she kept it?"

I shook my head. "There was only a little left when she passed," I said. Feeling my nasty attitude swell, I couldn't resist adding, "*After* it sat for a year, I ended up throwing it away."

I let that statement sit and when he didn't volley back, I began feeling guilty, so I tried again. "I'm sorry, I didn't know you'd want it."

I thought I caught a flash of disappointment on his face before he shrugged. "It was probably for some of her hocus-pocus stuff anyway, but it seems... well, wrong not to have it. I guess I'm just as caught up in her insanity as I ever was."

I tried to overlook the way he disregarded his grandmother's faith. Usually, I'd have kicked someone out of my house who said such things, but I loved Gwen too much to let her grandson's final visit to her home be a negative one, even if her loved one was a prick.

"I'm sure I can find something with the scent on it, if that'll help."

He nodded, and I stood to go into Gwen's old bedroom to see if I could find anything he could take with him. I still considered it her room and had left it alone, not knowing if or when I'd have the heart to change it.

"I'm sorry, I didn't have any luck, but if you like, I can give you her recipe."

"Didn't she make that in her cauldron?" he asked.

"She did..." I told him, "...but if you're just wanting to capture her scent, you can just follow the recipe."

I knew when I said it, the guy probably couldn't fix his own dinner, much less cook up a complex potion from the distilled extract of flowers. But, that was for him to figure out.

He shook his head, and there was sadness in his eyes. I sighed inwardly. Those damned eyes were the same as his grandmother's and I'd never been able to say no to her. *Fuck*... I thought to myself as I relented. "If you're willing to stay the night, I could probably make the potion for you, but it needs several things from the garden, and will require you to spend some time here while I make it happen." He looked up, skepticism on his face, and I shrugged. "I understand. You'll probably want to be on your way. Shall I help you bring the chest down now?"

"I would like to have the vial. I don't buy into any of my grandmother's beliefs, but she always seemed to have that stuff around and it always smelled so fresh and floral. I'd like to have that as a way to remember her."

I bit my tongue, holding back all I wanted to say about the memories he could've created with Gwen had he ever visited. Still, I couldn't help the sigh that escaped my lips. "Well, let's go collect what we'll need then," I said, and went into the kitchen to get the big dishpan along with a couple smaller pots for ingredients.

I made him carry the pots as I harvested the flowers from Gwen's garden. I used the big pan for the nasturtiums, which bloomed prolifically. I popped one into my mouth and enjoyed the peppery flavor as it burst on my tongue.

"Did you just eat a flower?" Lance asked, sounding nonplussed.

I laughed. "You did grow up here, right?"

"Yeah, but I don't remember eating flowers."

"Do you like radishes?" I asked.

"Yeah, I guess, on a salad."

I plucked a nasturtium and handed it to him. "Make sure there are no insects inside, then eat it."

He stared at the flower for a moment, then, after looking inside, popped it in his mouth. As he chewed his eyes grew big and he smiled. "That does taste like a radish," he said.

I smiled back as I continued with the harvest. When I was done, I put the pan by the back door and picked up a small clay pot I loved to use for harvesting smaller things from the garden. We walked over to the roses blooming along the gate and western fence. When I began plucking the petals off the roses and sticking them into the pot, he exclaimed, "Why are you destroying the roses?"

I chuckled. "It's part of the recipe. Think of it as the sacrifice."

He shook his head and held the pot as I filled it to the brim. I always loved the way petals looked when mixed together, with the different shades of pink, burgundy, white and red. I kept my nostalgia to myself, though, as I doubted this hulking man would share my reverie for something so delicate.

I could tell he was fed up with my garden harvest and was becoming antsy, so I asked him to go inside and get us both a glass of lemonade from the kitchen.

He and his brothers were raised in this house, so I figured he didn't need instructions on where to find the glasses, even if it had been ages since he'd set foot in the place.

I finished gathering the flowers I needed, and sat down at the tandem swing Gwen and I had enjoyed sitting in after working in the garden. Lance came out with two glasses of lemonade, handed one to me, and sat on the other side of the swing.

"So, how did you and my grandmother meet?" he asked.

I shrugged. "We were both attending an event in Kansas several years ago and hit it off. I came out to visit her a couple times and fell in love with this area, so I let her persuade me to move here."

Lance looked at me strangely. "I never understood your relationship," he said candidly.

I laughed. "There wasn't much to understand. We were friends, then when this place got to be too much for her to manage *alone*..." I emphasized while making eye contact with him, wanting him to see my displeasure with his never being around, "...we became roommates. If you'd ever come to visit, you'd have known that."

The venom in that last statement shocked even me. I guess seeing how much it hurt Gwen that her grandsons were so estranged had really gotten to me. I knew it couldn't have been because of her, she was a polite, caring, and loving person. If there was a problem between this man and his grandmother, it was all on him.

He ignored the jab, and said, "I wasn't all that surprised when she sold you the house. None of us wanted it anyway, and she put the money in a trust for us. I went through all the paperwork at the time, and you even gave her a fair market value, which saved me from having to come after you for taking advantage of an elderly woman."

Before I even had time to think, I jumped up to leave, nearly spilling my lemonade I was so pissed. I wouldn't be accused of anything, not in my own home, and certainly not by this prodigal grandson who had never returned. I also owed him zero explanations of my relationship with Gwen. "Maybe you should go now. There's a motel in town where you can stay for the night," I said. "I'll make the potion and you can pick it up tomorrow morning before you leave."

"Wait," he said. "That came out wrong. We were all worried about her living out here alone. The coast is extremely rural and without many services for the elderly, and drug activity has increased tremendously over the past decade. We were all just worried she'd accidentally gotten involved with the wrong kind of person."

I sighed, willing myself to stay calm.

"Mr. Franklyn, we should get something straight. I never took advantage of your grandmother. I paid her rent until I purchased the home from her, then she paid me rent. We both agreed that nothing as ridiculous as finances should impede our friendship. You don't know what our agreements were, because you weren't ever here to find out. That hurt your grandmother, and because it hurt her, I am a bit prickly about you." Lance looked like he was about to respond, so I put my hand up to stop him, and continued, "Your issues are none of my business, and my relationship with your grandmother is none of yours, so I'll keep my nose in its place if you'll do the same with yours. Are we agreed?"

The way Lance looked at me, I could tell he wanted to argue. Maybe he'd come to pick a fight, but I was in no mood to play his or anyone's games, especially since it'd been more than a year since my dear friend died, and I'd yet to see this man act like he gave a damn.

He nodded, and I took a deep breath, and continued, "Okay, so here's how this needs to go. Your grandmother always used the moonlight to create this potion. We have about a half hour before the sun sets, so I can help you bring the chest down from the attic, then we can go get set up for the spell."

He squinted at me, and I could tell he wanted to ask me about the spellcasting, but I turned to head in through the back door before he had the chance. As he followed me silently into the house, I mumbled to myself, "I love you, Gwen, but I'll be happy to see the back of this one!"

Damn, I'd known this man was going to be trouble, but I had hoped the banishment charms I'd scattered around the property to keep tourists away would push him on his way quickly and efficiently. They clearly hadn't been strong enough to fully keep him at bay. I should've known it wouldn't be that easy to keep Gwen's family from showing up. I could almost hear Gwen chuckling at ever thinking it could. Not that I really wanted to keep him or his brothers away. No, I needed them to get their shit, so I could move on, and maybe so could she. Jeez, even now the anger level in me was at boil.

I shook all of that off, reminding myself this was Lance's chance to say goodbye, and I had no business interfering with that. So, after getting the chest out of the attic, I walked out the back door. When Lance followed, I handed him the crystal pitcher to collect the water from the stream running through the property, down by the place Gwen liked to sit at night.

I led the way with the other supplies we'd need and set them on the picnic table next to Gwen's old cauldron. I'd kept it seasoned and ready for use, although I didn't need a cauldron for my spellcasting. I preferred to work directly with herbs in the fire, but of course, I never made potions or other such things. That was her specialty.

I turned the iron cauldron over and attached it to the three metal supports, then walked him down to the stream to fill the pitcher.

We came back, poured the water into the cauldron, and I chanted a cleansing spell over it to prepare for the spells to come.

I sent him back to refill the pitcher while I worked on preparing the other spell supplies.

"So, you're Wiccan?" Lance asked as I was working on preparing for the spell.

"No, your grandmother was, though. I'm a mixture of several things. I appreciate Wicca, but my way of practicing is a mix of a lot of different approaches to Goddess worship."

He shook his head like he didn't quite understand and didn't really want to, so I let the subject drop, and put the final elements on the table.

"Your grandmother had an affinity for this particular potion, using it for a variety of purposes, including as a tea she drank, as well as to shift the energies when she made her famous love potion. It's similar to this one, but has a few more ingredients. She also showed me how to use the liquid for scrying, to see the future of a person's potential love life. It... well, it was something she tended to use for a variety of different things."

I chuckled internally at how her coven had hated that, arguing with her that she needed to create different potions for different things. Gwen was one of a kind though, and her magic always worked like it should, so her "one size fits all" potion seemed to work... at least for her.

When Lance nodded at me sadly, I just let things drop, not that he cared much about the magical properties of things anyway. Gwen had taught me how to make the brew when she became too sick to do it herself.

Luckily, despite my affinity being more along the lines of air magics, I'd always had a special way with herbs, and when I fixed the potion for her, she complimented me on my skill.

"I just don't understand why you need to make it in this great iron cauldron. It's just for effect, right?" he asked.

I sighed. "Lance, you're a skeptic. Even when your grandmother was alive, she'd laugh about how you were the grandchild who resisted her ways the most. I can tell you why she probably used the cauldron, but I doubt it'll have much relevance to you, but for now, I need you to trust me. Can you do that at least?" I asked.

He nodded sullenly, then skulked away and sat on the chair Gwen used to sit by her fire at night when she wanted the breezes from the ocean waves to flow over her.

I was probably being insensitive. He'd asked me to make the potion for him, and I was happy to. I loved the smell of it, and Gwen used it so often, it was quintessentially her scent. The light floral aroma certainly made me think of her.

After I wiped out the water I'd used to cleanse the cauldron, I laid the deep clay vessel inside, basically creating a type of distillery inside the cauldron. That wasn't quite right, since we weren't really making alcohol, but the effect was the same. Gwen had made the clay vessel herself for this purpose. I filled the vessel with river rocks to keep it weighed down. Gwen had also made a smaller pot that sat perfectly on top of the other to collect the distilled liquid from the flower water.

I was sort of glad Lance had walked away. There was no denying the guy was a pleasure to look at, inheriting his grandmother's striking features, her big, beautiful eyes especially, that seemed to glow when he looked at me. Still, no matter how good-looking he was, I hated working around a skeptic, and would've forced him to leave under normal circumstances. Goddess, I was such a wuss, but I figured he had a right to his grandmother's recipe, even if I had to force him to trust me enough to do it right.

The wind had picked up slightly. The smells of the garden swarmed around me, and I couldn't help but smile. This had become Gwen's way to announce her presence, and I was keenly aware her spirit was with us.

Usually, I would've spent the entire day cleansing the cauldron before working with it. Any good practitioner would tell you not to use someone else's tool without cleaning it of their energy first. I suspected, however, that Gwen's energy was as important as any ingredient for this potion. I was simply a vessel tonight to channel the woman's power for this last hurrah for her grandson.

Nasturtiums, of course, were the main ingredient, which gave the brew a delicious smell and nice burn when you drank it.

"Power from the garden grows, created with the Goddess's glow, we bring you here to bless this brew with knowledge given to but to a few."

I filled the bottom clay vessel with the nasturtiums we'd harvested earlier.

Next, I found the rose petals. We were lucky it was early fall and the roses had just grown a flush of new blooms as they did this time of year. Gwen preferred the one-time bloomers with a more historical quality to them. She especially liked the varieties from eighteenth-century France and had a cabbage rose she swore came from the Versailles gardens grown by Marie Antoinette herself.

There was probably an intentional irony to the fact that Gwen's garden also sported several varieties from Josephine Bonaparte. Luckily, some of these included a few repeat bloomers.

"French roses have the most romance in them," I could hear her lecturing me even as I was looking at the rose petals.

I assumed she also liked the meaning behind having roses from such notorious French monarchs, both with different histories, but similarly sad love stories.

"Let these petals fall and float, among the other flowers note, their powers be but first in love, but follows fast with protective glove. I fill this brew with love and light, to fight off the dark that flows with spite."

I poured the rose petals in on top of the nasturtiums. Just as I had when Gwen showed me, I could feel the energy in the area shift. That was my cue to bind the circle.

"Energy flow is dangerous if not properly wielded," Gwen had warned me. My own Christian grandmother had told me a similar thing when I was a child. She practiced a form of witchcraft herself, but if anyone had accused her of that, she'd have been incensed.

I poured salt around the circle, and when I came to the point that would've excluded Lance, I hesitated. "She wants you to be a part of this," I said, ignoring the skeptical look he gave me. "Can you bring the chair inside the circle and sulk in here?"

The man squinted his eyes at me, giving me a scathing look. I figured it was the same look he used when cross-examining a witness in court. After a moment of hesitation, though, he picked his chair up and stepped inside the circle, placing it next to the table where our ingredients were spread out.

When he sat back down, I lit a candle and, as Gwen had shown me, allowed the wax to bind the circle together where I'd joined the two salt lines.

It looked like Lance wanted to ask me something, but I winked at him and shook my head with a smile, placing my finger to my lips to keep him quiet. This wasn't the time for idle chitchat. The spell had begun, and it was important nothing interfered, especially the questions of a skeptic.

I added the rest of the flowers, a mixture of marigolds, mums, a daylily I found blooming in a hidden corner of the garden, bachelor's buttons, lavender, and a few dandelions I found lurking as well. According to Gwen, the additional flowers didn't matter so much. They were fillers, there to add flavor and beauty. Of course, each flower had its own power and purpose when used in spells, but for this recipe, we weren't calling on them to play a starring role.

"Mix and match, piece and patch, these flowers I add to blend this batch."

I heard the scoff next to me, and without looking at him, I waved my hand, making a circle in the air to silence him literally and figuratively. When I turned around, I could see the shock on his face when he was no longer able to make a sound. It was for his own good, really. Inside the circle, I had more power over others than I normally would've, and I needed him to remain quiet for just a few more moments.

I poured the rest of the flowers into the cauldron, then released the spell that kept the man silent.

"Would you like to pour the water in?" I asked.

When I was met with a menacing stare, I said, "If you continue to send negative energy toward me, I *will* dump this on the ground. I will not be a part of creating a negative potion, so you can either clean up your energy or we'll be done, understand?"

Lance nodded and even though he should've been able to speak now, he remained silent.

He stood and walked toward me, and I could sense his energy had indeed shifted. That was surprising in and of itself. In my mind, I credited Gwen since she had little to no tolerance for negative energies thrown at her by sulky children or adults.

I handed him the huge crystal pitcher containing the water he'd gathered from the stream. The stream was a salmon run, and I'd swear I saw several when we'd first filled the pitcher. That boded well for the spell as far as I was concerned. Nothing signified the sacrifice around love and procreation more than the epic annual migration of salmon to spawn in a place that protected their young.

I directed Lance to pour the water over the flowers only, and not into the top vessel. "We will be collecting the distilled potion in this section," I said, so he understood where I wanted the water to go. Next, I added a few essential oils to where the water would condense, as well as a couple other things Gwen had shown me belonged in the mix. Then, I put the inverted lid on the cauldron.

I bent down to light the fire under it when Lance finally used his voice, to ask, "How long will this take?"

"About an hour," I answered. "Just long enough to force the water to evaporate, then condense on the lid."

He nodded, then asked, "What's the ice for?"

"That comes after we get the fire going. We add it to the lid to help the condensation process. It's just a little modern cheat to help things progress. It reduces the time we have to wait for the magic to happen."

He looked at me oddly as I finished speaking. "I thought you all didn't like that word—*magic*," he said.

I laughed. "You can call it whatever you like. I don't have a problem with that word, but yeah, some do."

"Grandma said it wasn't that she disliked it. She just said it wasn't... accurate."

"I agree. Magic implies you can do or get something for nothing. Like asking a genie for a wish. Spellcasting and other prayers or energy work is more about shifting things and require giving something in return."

He turned then like he was going to leave the circle. "Oh no, you can't break the circle yet. It's important to stay until the deed is done, otherwise, it could go awry."

He just shook his head. "I shouldn't have asked you for all this. I just thought you'd mix up some stuff and I'd have her scent again. I didn't anticipate all the hooey that goes with it."

"Your grandmother was a witch, and she was a dear friend of mine," I chastised him. I'd had about all I could take of his sarcasm. "I would never just do her spell without all the proper respect it requires. You should respect her at least the same, if not more, Lance. You don't have to agree with, or even believe in, her ways to be respectful of them."

The man made me angry. I shouldn't have let him have that much power, but I wondered how someone as sweet and committed to the craft and the natural order as Gwen could've had a hand in raising someone as... well, as opposite in a grandson. I had to draw in several deep breaths, allowing the positive energies we'd created by the spell to fill me back up and drive out the negative ones I seemed to have absorbed from him.

I ignored him until the fires were burning under the cauldron enough to make the water in the flower mixture boil.

"Add the ice to the top of the lid now, if you don't mind."

Lance did as I requested while I stood directly across from him and closed my eyes. I allowed my third eye to focus, then looked out over the circle.

Gwen was there smiling at me. *You know he's just being difficult because he doesn't understand all this*, she said, communicating telepathically like we'd been doing since she'd passed away.

You shouldn't have influenced me to invite him, I replied. *He could've thrown the entire spell off. Who knows what we've created in that potion?*

She chuckled. *You've created something beautiful, and you know it. I can feel it on this side, which is an accomplishment, you know.*

Well, no, Gwen. I'm still alive, so I don't know, but I'll take your word for it.

You are still a total brat! She smiled despite her chastisement. *You got him to trust you, that was no small feat, and it's as important to what you've done today as the potion itself. By the way, you'll need to keep half of the potion for yourself,* she told me then. *Half for you, half for him.*

I eyed her suspiciously. *What are you up to, Gwen?*

She put her hands up in front of her. *This isn't just from me. There's darkness moving in the distance, and it's got unpleasant written all over it. It wishes harm to both you and Lance. Trust me, this isn't just a love spell. The thorns of the rose are protective as much as the flower is beautiful.*

I nodded. *Not just a love spell. I know your trick, Gwen Franklyn. But just so you know, I'm immune to your love spells, so stop trying to fix me up. Besides, as much as I love you, I have no interest in getting involved with your Neanderthal kin!*

Gwen cackled. *You aren't being very open-minded,* she replied. *But you and I both know, no love potion can force you to fall in love. Neither can it save you from heartache. The best this can do is show you what you're in for if you decided to pursue a relationship with him, and even that's unlikely with your pitiful scrying skills!*

I stuck my tongue out at her, and she laughed again as she disappeared from my vision.

When I opened my eyes, Lance was studying me carefully. "You seemed to be in a trance."

"I sort of was. It's time to pull off the water and add more ice," I said with an effort to distract him from asking more questions. I used the old ladle Gwen had kept for the purpose, and scooped out most of the water.

When I was done, I motioned for Lance to pour more ice on the lid.

I didn't look with my third eye again. Gwen had left, I could tell by the empty feeling in my heart. As much as I thought the woman should transition, I was glad we could hang out a few more times at least, even if she was still playing matchmaker.

Once the ice melted, I announced we were done with the spell. I pulled my athame out of my belt and used it to cut the circle. I was happy to use Gwen's tools for everything but this. When it came to managing energy circles, I preferred and trusted my own tools.

When I turned around, Lance was standing behind me. "You believe all this stuff, don't you?" he asked.

I chuckled. "You did, too, a half-hour ago when you couldn't talk."

"That's some kind of hypnosis. I learned about all that in school. You can make people do something with the power of suggestion."

"Believe what you like," I said and went back to the cauldron to remove the lid and collect the potion.

It smelled heavenly. It was a particularly strong batch, stronger than the few times I'd made it for Gwen. I assumed that was because I had an active spirit from the other side working on the spell with me.

I poured the liquid into waiting vials I'd cleansed and blessed a couple nights before when the moon was full. Intuition had told me they'd be needed in the next moon cycle, and my intuition had been correct.

Once the vials were full and sealed, I handed one to Lance and said, "There ya go."

"What are you going to do with the other?" he asked.

"Your grandmother told me I should keep it. I guess we need to be prepared as something wicked this way comes."

"My grandmother?" he asked, surprised. "Um, man, I hate to tell you, but she's no longer with us."

I just shook my head. "Whatever you say, but keep that secure, nonetheless. It may come in handy over the next few months."

I poured the ice water on the now-dying coals, and had Lance help me collect the supplies around the cauldron to return to the house.

"I'll deal with the cauldron and inner pots tomorrow once they've had time to cool," I assured him.

When we got back to the house, I told him to take any of the upstairs bedrooms for the night. I'd taken the one downstairs across from Gwen's when she'd become ill, and hadn't moved into the master bedroom after she'd gone. It just felt more like she was still here when I was across the hall from where she used to sleep.

"Wait, I appreciate what you did. This is just difficult for me. I avoided it as long as I could."

"There's no hard feelings," I lied as I walked back toward my bedroom.

"Um, if you're hungry," he said behind me, "I'd be happy to spring for a pizza, which, unless things have changed, is about the only thing you can get this time of night around here."

I thought about declining, then I thought about what Gwen would've wanted.

I turned around and stared at him a moment. "I don't especially like you, Lance. You're arrogant and contemptuous about what your grandmother and I believe.

Not to mention you just showed up unannounced, as if I owe you something, which I do not, by the way. I realize you hold a powerful position with the state government, and if you wished, you could probably make things difficult here since we're a small town. If you want to share a pizza with me, I'm happy to oblige, but you may not accuse or insinuate I misused my relationship with your grandmother, you may not disrespect me or my faith, and you will be polite to me, which includes no more scoffing. Is that agreeable?" I asked, half expecting him to say no.

Instead, he took a deep breath and nodded. "You're right. I've been an ass since I arrived. I apologize."

"Then, you may use the landline to call the pizza place. Your cellphone won't work here," I said, and let that statement linger, wanting him to understand it was my choice that neither his nor any mobile device worked here. "They close in an hour, so you'd better get your call in now if you want Godfrey to have time to deliver it. He has a strict no-delivery policy after nine o'clock. After a bunch of stupid, drugged-up kids who'd been visiting town tried to jump him after hours, he stopped offering that service."

Without another word, Lance walked over to the phone and called, while I went into my room and got my wits about me. I would need to figure out how to be polite myself. If I was going to let this man into my life, even for the night, I'd have to find some sort of forgiveness for him and his brothers. Was it possible? For Gwen's sake alone, I'd try.

Four

Lance

I PICKED UP THE phone as I watched the sexy, angry, frustrating man walk out of the living room and toward what I assumed was his bedroom... the same bedroom that had once been mine, not that it mattered. Any claim I'd once had to that room, this old house, or to being part of this small town, all belonged to the past.

I'd been a jackass though, I could admit that. I mean, I was a fucking politician, I knew how to play nice, even if just for the cameras. Even the hand full of times I'd had to cross paths with my grandparents and mom... ugh, that'd been hard, almost impossible, but I'd managed to remain civil.

Somehow, Drew Andreassen pushed every button I had. I'd openly scoffed at his religious beliefs, insulted him, and questioned his relationship with my grandmother, and yet he had somehow done what I couldn't. He'd been respectful, even cordial, albeit in a cold, icy way.

I placed the order, and since Drew was nowhere in sight to ask what toppings he wanted, I got the same ol' cheese pizza my brothers and I had always ordered from

Godfrey's, because it was the only kind we all liked. Of course, that was probably more evidence of me being an ass... at least I was paying for it.

The pizza arrived, and I sat across the kitchen island from Drew as we both silently ate. His icy demeanor had not changed. Not that I really blamed him. Not only had I been a jerk all afternoon and evening, but he was right. My brothers and I hadn't been there the last few years of our grandmother's life. My daughter Jennie had even come to visit, and she had nailed me on numerous occasions about not coming down to see Grandma.

Jennie was more like her great-grandmother than she should've been, considering they had only seen each other a smattering of times. The few occasions Grandma had come to New York, Jennie had insisted that we all get together at her parents' house to visit. Of course, Grandma had loved her and her parents—my two besties—without question. She hadn't even batted an eye at my decision to be my friends' sperm donor, or our unconventional relationship that followed in raising Jennie. Grandma just took the love we all had for one another at face value.

I studied Drew for several moments before he finally made eye contact. I wanted to say something, wanted to ask questions about his life with my grandmother, wanted to know why he had been so attached to her. He looked as if he was about to speak, too, but as we stared awkwardly at one another, our mutual silence grew heavy.

Finally, Drew sighed and put his half-eaten slice of pizza down. "I'm going to bed, Lance, so if you need anything, just knock on my door, okay?"

I bowed my head, wanting to find some words to say that'd give us a little common ground, but they just wouldn't come. "Thank you," I said simply.

Once he was gone, I put our uneaten pizza in the fridge and went to sit in one of the chairs in the living room. All of the furniture had been replaced since I'd lived here. I'd almost expected to see the dated sofa and recliners I'd lounged on as teenager, but everything was clean, modern, and comfortable. Had Drew been the reason for the upgrade? The truth was, I didn't know, because I'd left. I'd gone away and stayed away, and had lost a lot more than all perspective about what this place had once meant to me.

I sighed and let it out slowly, surveying all the upgrades within view. I *had* called every Sunday like clockwork, letting myself believe my grandmother was never going to die and that I didn't need to travel to this hellhole, just because she was getting older. Hell, the woman was a witch. She should've had the power to keep herself alive, right?

It was all bullshit, and I'd all but convinced myself of that. We'd seen each other over the years, though she always traveled to see me and not the other way around. It wasn't like her house held bad memories either. On the contrary, the home was the happiest place from our childhood, not that I would classify that as a happy time, though.

Our parents had made us miserable. I'd avoided them since I... since *we* were kicked out all those years ago. They'd lived less than ten miles from our grandmother, who'd offered us refuge that night and with whom we'd lived until, one by one, we left for college. My parents had never come to visit, or spoken to me again. Good riddance for damned sure, but it didn't mean the rejection didn't still hurt.

Although my line of work sometimes required it, coming out to the coast was not my first choice, and if I could avoid it, I did. Unfortunately, for my sweet, loving, if not slightly insane grandmother, it meant I didn't visit like I should've.

I got up and wandered around the living room, and upon closer inspection noticed the personal items tucked here and there were a mix of Drew's and Grandma's. Just like when I'd been young, crystals of various sizes and colors—yellow, green, blue, white—were stowed in the corners of every windowsill. I recognized a few of them, remembering my grandmother telling me the names and significance of the different minerals when I'd been little.

Those were better days, good memories although fleeting, of when my dad had been happy. Even my stoic mother had been decent, or at least I think she had been. The truth was, after Dad kicked us out, I couldn't recall many memories of my parents at all, but perhaps that was a blessing of sorts. Sometimes I could grasp vague elements, like whispers at the edge of my mind, but what I did remember felt more like the stories of someone else's life.

I guess that was what surprised me most as I'd sorted through the things Grandma had left for me in the old chest. The items carefully packed inside brought up memories long-ago faded from my mind. The chest was full of sentimental things from my childhood, like the blanket I used to tote around when I was a toddler.

I could remember my mother saying she was going to throw it away when I'd outgrown it. I was maybe seven or eight at the time and was overwhelmed with the thought of losing the blanket. On a visit to Grandma's, I'd hidden it in the room I always slept in when we spent the night. Grandma had found it, maybe a month or so later and then had told me she was going to turn it into a larger quilt. Unfortunately, she never got around to it. Regardless, I smiled happily as I looked at the old thing, remembering how warm and snuggly—and *safe*—I'd felt wrapped in it when I'd been little.

My baby shoes were also in the chest, but I wasn't sure how she'd secured those. There were pictures of me and my brothers playing in the backyard, and on the beach below her home. Those were good days, and all three of us were laughing, which was rare after we'd been tossed from our parents' home.

There were also strange things I'd never seen before. Just like in the living room, there were crystals, along with pendants, and some stuff I assumed she'd just put into the chest and forgotten about.

There were a few valuables as well, but the most valuable item was probably the little wedding band that she'd placed in a wooden box Drew had given me when I'd come in. I had studied the ring as I sat in the attic. It used to be encrusted with four stones, but now only held one. No surprise, it was the diamond.

The memories were flooding back as I looked at it. "You are the diamond," Grandma used to tell me and point at it on her ring. "When you find the right one, this will belong to your husband." I wondered briefly why my grandmother hadn't given me the stone when I'd married Tom. Oh well, more fairytales.

"Grandma, I'm a boy, I'll marry a girl," I'd replied when she first told me. I think I was probably around five years old.

She just smiled and said, "Remember what I'm telling you." Okay, so she had some insight. That wasn't so unusual, right?

The little box that held the ring also had a piece of paper inside that read, *My beloved diamond.*

Seeing the ring and her handwriting sent a wave of grief through me, and I sat on the floor and cried for at least half an hour. I was surprised when Drew had left me alone, but I was certainly happy he had.

I was the big-bad attorney general, fair but tough. My nickname was Stoneman, because I could cross-examine and plead my cases without carrying the emotional baggage that got so many in my position into trouble. I wasn't supposed to have emotions in my line of work... unfortunately, locking them down in my personal life didn't serve me as well. That was why it'd taken me so long to come out here to begin with. I knew the moment I began digging into my grandmother's things, I'd be crushed like a bug underfoot.

It took some time for me to shake off the grief. Finally, I told myself to keep my wits about me. If someone, namely her weirdo roommate, snapped a picture of me and posted it to his social media accounts, my career would come undone pretty quickly.

Weird or not, though, I hadn't anticipated the roommate to be so fucking hot. Shorter than me, Drew was built like a swimmer—long and lithe, muscular but slim.

I could tell he wasn't someone who went to the gym like me. He probably spent most of his time working on the property, chopping wood and stuff like that.

I'd always had questions about him. *Who was he? Why was he here?* There was never a good reason for a young man like him to want to live with an old woman, unless he intended to take advantage of her. I'd run his records when I'd first heard about him, and he was clean even on the federal database, which we weren't supposed to access unless it was important. Well, my grandma *was* important.

Despite my intense mistrust of him, I couldn't find anything to justify my gut feelings, but that didn't mean there wasn't plenty to be found.

I'd ended up hiring a private investigator who told me my grandmother and Drew shared the same beliefs. The investigator had given me a strange look, and let it be known he thought their religion was distasteful, but he was hired as much for his discretion as his investigative skills. The governor himself had recommended the guy to me.

The only thing of note we found was that Drew's father had been suspected of child abuse, but no charges against him had ever stuck. After that, I pretty-much gave up. I figured there were secrets, but my grandmother was a strong-willed person. If something went down, I could help her pick the pieces up later and maybe convince her to sell her property on the coast and move to the city, closer to me.

She had told me when she'd sold the property to her roommate and put the significant proceeds into a trust, though she hadn't explained why. I wondered how the man could afford to purchase the land and house in such a desirable area, but that really wasn't my business, at least not unless he was arrested and charged with a crime, *then* it *would* be my business, and I fantasized about prosecuting the substitute grandchild to the fullest.

The thought caused me to sigh and shake my head. I knew my low opinion of Drew was fueled by jealousy, but to be honest, that didn't bother me much. With two siblings, I'd learned how to recognize and manage jealousy from a young age. What was one more in the line of competition?

My contempt slipped out after I first arrived, and while we were sitting on the tandem swing, I was afraid I'd gone far enough that he was going to kick me out. He sure had every right to. I didn't mean to accuse him, but I was so angry he'd been the one to spend the last few months, days, and moments of my beloved grandmother's life with her. I hadn't even known she was sick. She hadn't told me or my brothers.

It should've been us—actual family—with her as she transitioned out of this world, not some interloper. I'd decided to show up unannounced on purpose. I guessed I was hoping to find him involved in something illegal. Instead, I found a quiet man who was clearly enjoying a cup of tea and a novel when I arrived. He'd been cordial and kind, which had rubbed me the wrong way even more.

My crying in the attic had just made me angrier at myself for not having been here for Grandma. By the time I'd gone to the backyard, I wanted to pick a fight with Drew, and he looked like a good target. I was wrong.

The man was an brick wall, and I realized quickly he could easily toss me aside and go about his life.

I wasn't ready for that either. I found myself wanting to know more about him, about his life with my grandmother. I wanted to know about her final moments, and if she'd had any last wishes, and only he had those answers. I shook my head again, frustrated with myself. Why couldn't I just ask him? I'd never been afraid of asking hard questions. My experience as an attorney had honed that skill, but for whatever reason, as the sexy man sat across from me at dinner, I just didn't know how to broach this subject.

Maybe guilt was tying my tongue.

With dinner long over, I lay on the bed staring at the ceiling. I let out a heavy sigh as I contemplated how much I'd fucked up this visit. I'd worked hard not to be derisive over the whole spellcasting thing. I'd seen enough of it when I moved in with my grandmother, and it always seemed so unnecessary to me, like showing off or something. To the be fair, though, I thought Christianity was just as ridiculous. All the lighting candles and ritualistic stuff just wasn't my thing. I believed there might be a divine power, but I'd been in law long enough to see religion, whatever it was based on, was more often than not used as a weapon or excuse for illegal behavior.

When I scoffed during the spell, I'd been surprised when he'd hypnotized me well enough to keep me quiet. Of course, it hadn't lasted long, which confirmed it was likely just a parlor trick. It was an impressive one, though, and I admired his ability to deal with me, even though I was admittedly being a dick. I'd have loved to learn how to do his hypnosis thing, as I'd love to shut up a variety of people I had to deal with in court or even at the office.

It was probably best not to know for the sake of my career, though, as I was sure I'd use it on the governor, or some loose cannon representative, given the chance.

FIVE

—·—

DREW

DESPITE MY INFURIATING AND awkward evening with Lance, I slept deeply that night. At first, my dreams were of flowers that would've made the flower children of the nineteen sixties proud.

I wasn't sure when the dream began to turn.

I was riding a wave of psychedelic flowers one moment, and the next I was in total darkness. The figure standing across from me was foreboding and intimidating. I couldn't make out his face, but I knew he was related to Gwen and Lance.

"You will not interfere," a menacing voice said, and at first, I couldn't tell if it came from the figure or someplace else.

"Why are you here?" I asked, then heard laughter.

"I'm always with him. He will never be rid of me."

I shuddered. I could feel the malice, and knew this entity was wrong, like a darkness when it should be daylight.

I waved my arm, smelling Gwen's scent on my hands, and I knew then who I was speaking to. "You're Gwen's son."

I felt more than heard the sneer. "I'm no one's son."

I shook my head. It was right, it wasn't a whole entity. It was a broken piece, something gone wrong. As I looked closer, I could see the spell that bound it.

I knew better than to speak with an entity created by dark magic, so I quickly surrounded myself with my own energy, essentially blocking it from me.

Before I closed the circle, I heard its malicious laughter. "You'll never have him, he'll always be mine."

I woke up in a cold sweat, looked at the chair across from me, and saw Gwen sitting there.

"What was that?" I asked, but she didn't respond right away.

I leaned back against the headboard and closed my eyes, spreading the energy circle I'd created as a protection against the malicious spell to include Gwen.

When she was properly enclosed, I opened my third eye, so we could communicate easily without straining her.

What was that? I repeated.

Lance's father, she said sadly.

Why is Lance's father a cantation?

Lance should tell you, it's his story, but since he has chosen to attack you, I will tell you it was a curse gone wrong.

Lance's father cursed him?

She nodded, sadness showing on her face.

I see. Well, I'll need to prepare for battle then. It'll become dangerous now that it thinks I'm challenging it. Gwen just nodded. *Is his father dead?* I asked.

No, he's alive.

Good, then I'm not having to take on a cantation spirit combo.

No, but it's a powerful force nonetheless. I was never able to overcome it.

It wasn't for you to overcome. That book you had from your husband's great-grandmother, Brumheilda, the one on cantations, I've read it and I'm sure you have as well. You know as well as me those nasty things are usually associated with their victims. He'll have to overcome it. Or, in this case, they'll have to. It's too powerful for just one person.

She nodded. *It's all his children. He cursed all of them at the same time.*

Well, fuck, I said. *Gwen, this isn't good. You should've told me.*

She smiled at me sadly. *It wasn't my story to tell. It's theirs.*

I studied her for a moment. *There's more you haven't told me. I can see it in your face.*

I've suspected you were somehow involved for some time, but until tonight I wasn't certain. If the cantation came to you directly, it sees you as a threat. I've been adding my protections to yours, but even my help won't keep you from having to face this again. I highly recommend you befriend my grandson. The only way you'll find peace is with him by your side.

I laughed. *That isn't happening,* I said, but when she didn't share in my amusement, I sobered quickly. *Well, that's fucking great. How do I keep letting you get me into these things?*

Usually, my dear friend would smile or laugh, but this time she shook her head. *It's because you're linked to me. I'm sorry, Drew.*

She faded from my sight, and I got up shaking my head. "Fuck me," I said out loud. "Just fuck me!"

The next morning, I sat across from Lance at the kitchen table, eating a breakfast of vegan pancakes and fruit. I caught his slight grimace when I plopped the food in front of him, but after digging in, he moaned approval like he hadn't eaten in a week.

"So, tell me about your father," I said as he shoveled the last bite into his mouth.

The choking sound he made was a balm to my tiredness, compliments of the night of no sleep and my horrible attempt to scry what I was up against, which, incidentally, I'd failed at miserably. Gwen was right, I really sucked at all things divination.

"Um, why do you ask?"

"'Cause, apparently, the man has a habit of visiting people who've graciously invited you to stay with them and threatening them in the middle of the night."

Worry raced across his face before he schooled it. "I'm sure my grandmother has told you about my father..." he began, and I waved him off.

"You and I both know your grandmother would do no such thing. She'd think it was a violation of your privacy. Considering the woman guarded hers like a dragon guarding its treasure, if you knew her at all, you'd know I'm not lying."

I waited for him to agree, and although he certainly didn't do so verbally, I could see it on his face.

"So, back to the reason I was awoken from a lovely dream of psychedelic flowers and thrust into a threatening nightmare with your father as the bad guy." He cleared his throat, and I knew it was to stall for time. "Counselor, your tricks aren't going to work on me. I already know them before you start. Spill!"

He smiled at my comment for a moment, then sighed. "My father isn't a good man," he began, and I watched his face to make sure he was telling me the truth. I might suck at divination, but I could read people well. "When I was young, he tossed my brothers and me out of our home when we all came out as gay or bisexual."

I nodded. "Yes, Gwen did tell me that much. I'm sorry about that, by the way. Unfortunately, it happens to way too many children."

At his silence, I resumed eating, and when I looked back up at him, he was staring at me. All my anger was gone, and only empathy remained. I'd actually forgotten about his history. Now I felt like a total shit bringing it up.

"Okay, now I feel bad, so I won't force you to talk, but I need to tell you what your father said last night, or at least something that came from him. 'You'll not interfere.' It wasn't a question, it was a demand, and if I attempted to interfere, I felt it would do me harm. Then, I spoke to your grandmother, and she told me you and your brothers had been cursed, but she didn't give me details, said it was your story to tell. Lance, I know you like to avoid the gifts you have. I also know you have them. I know your grandmother was a gifted witch, although she wasn't born into a magical family, but if I'm in danger because your father, or at least your father's cantation, is coming for me, I should know what I'm up against."

He shook his head. "First, what the hell is a cantation? Second, I honestly don't know whether you're throwing my grandmother's stories at me, or if you really believe what you're saying. What I do know, though, is I should be going."

I shook my head as he began to get up from the table. I guessed I knew that was how he was going to react.

"A cantation is like an eidolon," I said, which prompted him to sit back down, though he still wore a blank expression. "It's an entity that exists outside of someone, like a spirit, or shade, but the person can still be alive. We use a cantation to describe something that's associated with a curse or spell. It's like incantation, but of course... it's the element that becomes... because of the spell..."

Lance continued to look blank, clearly unmoved, so I just went on, "You're welcome to leave, Lance, but here's what's going to happen. You're going to start having nightmares, and yes, I know you've already begun having them, probably since your father cast whatever curse or spell he did on you. Unfortunately for me, we are now somehow linked, probably thanks to your meddling grandmother and her love potions, which incidentally, I think we brewed last night, so I'll have the pleasure of sharing those with you. Along with your nightmares, if you leave this too long, you're probably going to get physically sick. I feel that you and I are both air energy.

That means we draw most of our energy from the air around us. When we avoid or block energy, it usually manifests itself in poor health and lack of vitality."

His expression morphed into one of disbelief, which didn't surprise me, but he needed to understand what we were facing, so I continued, "It won't be diagnosable, but you'll feel awful. The spell we worked last night will work against the curse from the past... but if you don't face it, I'm certain it will manifest itself as illness. Before you get upset, know I'm going to be suffering here as well. It's unclear since I'm not the one who was cursed, but as I said before, now that we're linked, I'll have the horrible benefits of dealing with anything residual from you." I shook my head. "So, go on, hide in your big office in the state capital, but when you're ready to face this shit, give me a call, or better yet, just come on by, since you apparently like to visit people unannounced."

With that, I got up, put the dishes in the sink, and walked toward the back door. "When you're ready to leave, please make sure to push the lock button on the front door knob on your way out." I walked out of the house and left the man to his own thoughts. *Fuck.* "Gwen, you've gotten me into a fucking mess!" I said out loud.

I walked around the back of the house and up the path that led to my neighbor's place. The woman was a hedge witch, meaning she could see the future much better than me. As usual, I was met by the protective charms placed around the property. I pushed slightly against them and waited. When I felt them give, I smiled. There was never a greeting sweeter than a hedge witch dropping her protective circle to let you in.

I walked up to the front gate, and was immediately met by the beautiful woman whose gowns flowed around her mysteriously. Alegia loved being a witch, and wrapped herself in clothes that announced her faith rather than hid it.

She kissed my cheek as I came close and welcomed me. "Drew, to what do I owe the honor?" she asked, and I chuckled.

"You mean to tell me you don't already know?"

She shook her head. "Dear neighbor, you know the rules, you must ask for help before I can give it."

"In that case, can you help?"

"A little," she sighed, "...but not as much as you'd like."

"You know she led me right into this, like a freaking trap?"

Alegia and Gwen had been rivals of sorts. Whereas Gwen was a witch who practiced as part of a large coven, the largest one in the Pacific Northwest in fact, Alegia was in every way a hedge witch, meaning she kept mostly to herself.

Alegia's husband was a Kel—the people who lived in the great forest. As far as I knew all the Kels were air elementals, and since Alegia, like most hedge witches, was earth energy, they proved an interesting yet powerful couple. They had a daughter named Scarlett who was a live wire, a perfect mix of her reserved father and extraordinary mom.

Alegia chuckled. "I think it was always in the cards, but her grandson took his time before he set the clock ticking."

"You know I don't buy the destiny stuff, Alegia. We—"

She interrupted me. "I know, we create our own destiny, but that doesn't mean people aren't put in our path for us to meet. This man has been squarely in yours for as far back as I can see, and you know that's far, Drew... very far!"

"No one will ever accuse you of being modest, Alegia!"

She ignored me and led me into the house, and I knew without instruction I was to follow her.

The house was deserted, which was no surprise. Alegia would've predicted I was coming and probably asked her family to give us space before I arrived.

There were many ways of divination. Some involved looking into water or mirrors called scrying, while others involved cards, dice, or runes. A large bowl of water sat on the table, and I knew instantly it was going to be scrying.

I sat across from the bowl, knowing that's where I'd be sent, while Alegia took her seat and gathered up several herbs she'd laid out on the table.

She sprinkled lavender, rosemary, and what appeared to be the petals of a marigold into the water, and stirred.

She stared into the water for a long time. I knew she was struggling when nothing seemed to happen. Usually when Alegia was scrying, her eyes tended to take on an aqua-blue glow. Finally, she sighed out of frustration, and said, "This is difficult. Whatever's blocking me is powerful, probably because it's the darkest of the dark—a parent betraying their child or children."

Standing, she went to her cupboard, and pulled out a large glass jar full of a dried herb. When she opened the lid, I knew by the smell that it was mugwort.

I cocked an eyebrow. Mugwort gave me wild dreams and not always good ones. Most divination practitioners rarely turned to the herb, because, although powerful, the visions that resulted tended to require more advanced skills to interpret.

Removing the large scrying bowl, Alegia placed a small cauldron on the table with a white candle in the bottom of it, then she lit the candle and let it burn. "If you want answers, I'm afraid we're going to have to go on a little journey. Have you done a guided dream quest before?" she asked.

"No, I haven't really needed to know my future until now."

"This will be a particularly difficult one, I'm afraid. You should know two things. First, what we're seeing is both real and not real. It's mostly images of what's happened, and those are often mixed with things that haven't yet occurred but... may. The future isn't linear, so we can only speculate what will happen, not really predict it. Second, unlike a dream, things can actually injure you in a dream quest. Being an air elemental makes it that much more dangerous. As you know, you are mostly spirit anyway, always lurking outside your body," she said, and smiled. "I will protect you as much as I can, but, Drew, you must do as I say, no going off on your own or ignoring me. When I tell you to do something, do it without thinking first."

She stared at me for a long moment before I nodded.

"Okay, let's begin." She took the mugwort out of the jar, and began to crumble it into the small cauldron while chanting in a language I didn't recognize.

The air around me became heavy and laden with malice, not unlike the dream I'd had the night before.

When she'd finished with the mugwort, she reached over and took my hands in hers. I saw the concern in her eyes from the quick change of energy in the room.

As she chanted, her eyes began to take on a glow as the room spun around me and eventually settled in a very nice home with high ceilings and stark décor. I saw a man with his hand raised and a young man at his feet. The image was still, as though we'd been transported to a particular time and place.

I heard Gwen beside me. "This is the moment it happened," she said. "This is right after he cursed them. He was angry because they came out. Well, no, not really. He was angry because he thought it would hurt his political campaign. I wish he'd sent them to live with me, but he had such strange expectations for those boys."

Gwen stared at the image for a moment before she put her hands on top of mine and Alegia's. When she did, the setting changed, and I was in another room. This time I saw two dark figures on a bed. I couldn't see them properly, only their silhouettes, but I blushed anyway. It was clear they were in the throes of sex. I turned then and saw Lance. He had clearly just walked into the room. The look on his face showed the horror anyone might feel finding a lover screwing someone else, but there was something else in his expression. Exhaustion mixed with resignation. My heart broke for the man.

The darkness then drifted in, and I felt the presence behind me.

As with my dream last night, I could feel the malevolence. It was angry. "You were warned," it growled, before reaching out a claw and swiping at me.

"Move!" I heard, and I jumped back just in time to avoid the worst of its attack, but not all. The claw scratched my arm.

It turned and rushed me again, but this time, Gwen was there. She held up her hand, and it froze, staring at her.

"Drew, run now!" I heard Alegia yell.

I did, without thinking.

As I crossed the threshold of the room, I was back with Alegia in her kitchen.

I reached over and felt the sting of the scratch on my arm.

When I looked, it was already festering and oozing.

"Shit," Alegia said. "Come with me."

She led me into the living room and hollered up the stairs, "Scarlett, come down now. I need you!"

Alegia's daughter dashed into the room quickly, and seeing my injury, rushed to a cabinet in the corner and began pulling our jars.

"Mom, make a poultice of camphor. I'll need fresh herbs for this. It looks... it looks not of this world," she said.

Her mom nodded, confirming it was a spiritual injury.

Scarlett rushed out, followed by Alegia, and I collapsed on a hardback chair next to the big fireplace. I didn't want to get oozing puss on their furniture, but I was quickly losing my ability to remain standing.

Within moments, both women returned. Chanting in the same language her mom had used earlier, Scarlett began to rub herbs into the poultice. Lights danced around the cloth, and I wondered if I was hallucinating, or if this was indeed part of the spell.

"Drew," she said, but it sounded like she was talking to me from a long way away. "Drew, this is going to burn, okay. Just let it sit for a moment to draw out the poison."

I nodded, but when they slapped the poultice onto the scratch, I heard myself screaming. It was like I was there and not there at the same time.

I realized then that I was floating above myself, watching the scene below me. I could see the cord that connected me to my body, and I could see the women working frantically to hold the poultice onto my arm. Then, I looked over as Frank, Alegia's husband, walked in. He looked up at me and frowned.

"Drew, you need to pull yourself back down into your body."

Alegia looked up at me then, and all but screeched, "Drew, get back in there now. This needs to be working on all of you, not just your body."

It was like I could hear them, but was unable to react. Frank walked over to where I floated and began chanting, and this time I understood the language. It was that of the Kels.

Within seconds, I was zapped back into my body, and the pain swept through me, making me nauseous.

The three moved me over toward the sofa and laid me down, then I must've passed out, because when I woke up, I was alone.

I looked down at my arm, and was surprised to see the poultice was gone, but so was the scratch.

I leaned up, but my head immediately began to swim. I laid back down, but yelled out, "Hello?"

Frank walked in and sat next to me. "Wow, you gave us quite a scare, neighbor."

I shook my head, and it swam again. "Um, what happened?" I asked.

Frank grimaced. "Apparently, you pissed off a rather nasty cantation."

"Where's Alegia and Scarlett?" I asked

"They're both asleep. I'm guessing I won't be seeing them again today. They had to work fast to stop the poison. Did you know what you were up against?" he asked, and I could feel the accusation.

I shook my head, but lightly this time. "No, this was sprung on me last night. I did a spell for Gwen's grandson, and it got me caught up in all this. I did see a cantation last night, but I didn't know it was this... well, this nasty."

"Good thing for you my wife and daughter were here to help. That thing meant to kill you. That's something you'll want to keep in mind from now on."

"It probably would've if it hadn't been for Gwen. She got between it and me."

"So, she hasn't passed over yet?"

"No, I knew she had something holding her back. Now I'm guessing it's this?"

Frank looked toward the empty fireplace for a moment. "I'm going to ask the Kels to come and cleanse your property. You're going to need more protection than Alegia and I can give you. I think you'll need the ancestors, especially since air is your power source. You need as much support as you can get."

I cleared my throat.

He turned back to me and smiled. "I'm sorry, Drew, I'm connecting with my people. They are already coming this way from the forest. Can you get home on your own?" he asked.

I tried to stand, but my head spun immediately.

"I didn't think so, but I need you home in your bed when they arrive. The smoke of our fires needs to surround your house, and probably mine now that the cantation has infected us as well."

He lifted me off the sofa and helped me back to my place. When we got to my bedroom, he said, "Strip down. You need to be unencumbered. Are your sheets cotton, or a mix with non-natural fibers?"

"No, I only use cotton."

"Good," he said and pulled my bed covers back, running his hand an inch or so over the sheets. "Yes, you did well here, it's all natural, even your mattress. That will allow you to absorb the protection we'll cast around you."

I lay down and vertigo made me feel as if I were going to throw up. He tsked then and left the room, only to return a moment later with a glass of water, and Gwen's potion from last night.

"I think you should drink this, Drew. It was practically vibrating on your counter."

"Thanks, Frank," I said, and added a few drops to the water and drank it.

My head immediately felt better, but I was overcome with exhaustion.

"Good, sleep now," he said. "You'll hear us more in your dreams, but don't be afraid, and don't try to get up, just let us do our job, okay?"

I nodded, and when he turned to go, I added, "Frank, I... thank you."

"Of course, Drew, you're our friend."

I lay back, gratitude washing over me. When Chemeketa was settled, there were fewer than ten tribespeople left in the area. The rest had been devastated by disease and wildfires. Nevertheless, they had easily integrated with the settlers here, their religion and the pagan religions perfectly complementing each other.

However, over time, the Kels, as we called them, had all but disappeared into the deep woods surrounding the town. With the rare exception of people like Frank, who fell in love with someone outside the tribe and moved into town, the Kels rarely associated with the rest of us. They were known as the air people, the ones who could sometimes be seen in the skies above Chemeketa. It was an intense honor that they would come out of the forest to perform a ritual for me.

I drifted off to sleep, probably before Frank had left. Before long, I could feel the Kels, singing and dancing in circles around the property. In my dream state, I saw smoke laced with spirits, the ancestors of the air people coming to help with the dance.

As the drumming became more intense, I began to see even more shapes in the smoke—an orca, primarily. It swam around me, around my home, and down by the stream. The orca represented the medicine person, the one who brought the cure. Mountain lion, bear, and ancient creatures I didn't recognize all followed where the orca had been.

When the salmon swam through the smoke, I could feel the air clear around me. That was when I felt Lance. After spending an evening with him, I knew him instantly. I doubted I'd ever mistake him again for anyone else. His strong, masculine energy permeated everything in his presence. I ignored the instant stir of attraction. The man was not my kind of lover. When I turned, he stood rooted in the middle of the clearing where the smokey salmon run had just swum seconds earlier.

He acted like he wanted to say something, and I smiled. The man used his mouth like a weapon. I assumed it probably was, and the thought sent sexual energy through my body again. He looked at me questioningly, and I winked at him, chuckling to myself at just how out of his element he was here. I turned from him and tumbled into a deep sleep, oblivious to anything else until I awoke late the next morning.

The area smelled of ozone, similar to after it rained following a drought. Petrichor, I thought it was called, but the air was clear, and the energies were all level and settled, which was strange since both Gwen and I were active practitioners, so we seldom had stable energies around us.

I snuggled into my bed, enjoying the peace. The image of Lance came back to my mind, his expression one of shock and frustration as he was surrounded by the tribe's energy. I hadn't known he was there until the last minute, but secretly I hoped he'd experienced the entire thing, not only because it was beautiful and healing, but because not even a skeptic could deny the power of it.

His expression after seeing my smile still held the frustration, but it held something else as well—a challenge... definitely, he was challenging me. He might not believe in the gifts, but there was no way that man was going to let me off the hook after last night. I figured things were about to get difficult for him anyway. The protection spells would certainly help him avoid the worst of it, but if he were actively pushing them away, they wouldn't be able to protect him for long.

I could feel Lance's impending return. I'd begin prepping for his arrival soon, after I'd paid Frank and Alegia a visit and thanked them for their help.

Regardless of when I had to deal with Lance—a definite question of when, not if—I needed to know why his father's cantation had attacked me in particular. I wasn't the source of the curse, but I'd somehow become a focus of it. That wouldn't work for long. As one of Chemeketa's leaders, it was up to me to keep the peace. I couldn't have a cantation plaguing me and causing energies to go awry. This had to be stopped sooner rather than later.

Six

—·—

Lance

My dreams were seriously bizarre during my first night back home in Salem. I tossed and turned as smoke floated around me. Somehow, I was both in my room and not. I caught glimpses of my grandmother's home in Chemeketa. Animals and humanoid figures danced around me, and I became lost in their movements, almost like I was being put into a trance.

When I saw Drew standing across from me, I immediately knew two things. One, I'd felt the stir of an intense attraction I'd never felt before, not even for my ex-husband. That overwhelmed me in and of itself. Deep down, I was a one-man guy, not in any way a player. I didn't like dating, and I generally didn't like meeting new people. What I liked was stability, and what I'd always wanted, but never had, was love.

With all my defense mechanisms down, when I looked at Drew, I saw that. Sexual appeal wrapped up in stability and love.

The second thing I knew was he was in my path. I couldn't avoid him, and I couldn't ignore him. Whether this dream was all his doing or not, he would have to be dealt with one way or another.

When I woke up, I thought about going back to Chemeketa to confront him, then I remembered the backlog of shit I had to get done before I announced I wasn't running for reelection, so I got up, dressed, and drove to the office.

I was immediately met by my secretary, who looked harried. "How do you already look like that? The week has only just begun?" I asked.

"The governor is in your office," she said, and I knew all of a sudden why she looked harried. I sighed, knowing I would have to face the music, and went to do so.

"Governor, it's a pleasure if not a surprise—" I said, so he could hear my frustration, "—to see you this early on a Monday morning."

When the door closed behind me, the man jumped up. "Lance, why the hell am I hearing through the fucking grapevine that you're not running for reelection?"

I shrugged. "I haven't told anyone I'm not running for reelection, governor. I'm not sure where you heard such a thing."

"You haven't announced your reelection campaign either, have you?" He looked surprised like he'd just gotten an epiphany. "Are you going to D.C. instead?"

I shook my head. "Governor, sit down a moment and let me have a rest before you start the inquisition."

My old friend did as I asked, but his inscrutable expression never left his face.

I put my things down on the desk, and asked for Judy to bring me and the governor a cup of coffee, since I usually did that first thing, and I had yet to have my morning hit.

When I sat down, I asked, "So, how's Melody?"

His eyes narrowed a bit, but the smile escaped anyway. "She's doing well, and wanted me to make sure, after yelling at you, I invite you over for dinner."

Judy brought the coffee in, put three creamers down for the governor, remembering how he drank his, and scurried back out the door.

"I'd love to come for a visit, if you still want me to after this conversation."

"Damn, Lance, I knew it."

I chuckled. "I'm not going to D.C. or New York, but I'm done with politics. So, to answer your question, no, I'm not running for reelection."

When he leaned forward, clearly getting ready to argue, I put my hand up. "Gerald, I'm tired. I've been running this intense rat race for too long. Recently, I've realized how much I hate politics. Yes, hate it!" I said, and the governor winced.

"I want a small practice to retire to, I want to travel, maybe spend some time in Europe when I'm not trying to figure out how to overcome a political crisis. My daughter is an adult now. She's grown up, and all I have are some piecemeal memories of her as a kid when I wasn't trying massive cases, or dealing with some high-profile client or politician who couldn't keep his dick in his pants. I'm sorry, but I'm done."

He leaned back, sipping his coffee before realizing it was still black.

"Blah, that's awful," he said, and reached over to begin pouring the half-and-half packets into his cup.

I chuckled. "You're a coffee wimp."

"I'm used to lattes these days. The younger generation has taught me to spoil myself. What can I say?"

"Nothing to me. I like mine bitter and plain. I haven't been converted to the froufrou coffee yet."

"We're the same age, Lance, and yet you feel like you could be my father!"

"So you've said."

I sighed, took a nice long drink of my coffee, and decided to dig in.

"I was going to tell you. In fact, my goal was to let you know by this Friday. I had a reporter digging around last week, wanting to know why I hadn't announced my reelection bid yet, since a few of my opponents have tossed their hats into the ring, and knew the day of reckoning was upon me, but I thought the son of a bitch would give me a few days before he jumped the gun."

"Twenty-four-hour news channels need massive amounts of information, even local news requires a constant fix. You should've known."

I heard the resignation in his voice.

"I'm thinking of running for president," he said. "I wasn't going to tell anyone, especially you, since my pushing you was one of the reasons why you came back home to Oregon to begin with, but now that you're resigning, I might as well let the cat out of the bag."

"You think that's a big secret."

He looked at me in astonishment. "You already knew?"

"Dude," I said, switching to what I'd called him when we were younger and roommates in college. "You're one of the most ambitious politicians I know. You're in your second term as governor and served in the Oregon Legislature before that. Anyone who knows you would know your next path is federal."

"I did think about running for the Senate, but I like our current senators, and the House just makes my head hurt."

I chuckled. Gerald Mumford was never a huge fan of governance by committee. He was an executive all the way. "The Senate might be okay, but seriously, you'd lose your mind in the House. Too many opinions and not enough brains."

That brought the smile back to his lips. "So, will you help with my campaign?"

I looked at him and knew. "So, this isn't you thinking about running, this *is* you running?"

He didn't say yes or no, but I saw the affirmation on his face.

"And Melody?" I asked.

"Ask her yourself, come to dinner this week. In fact, why don't you come this Friday? The kids will be there, and we're going to announce to them that I'm thinking about it."

"You want me there, so I can give you moral support when your daughters rip you a new one."

He stood and gave me the bright smile that always got him out of trouble. "They always have loved you."

"I'll be there," I said as I escorted my politician friend toward my door. "And tell your cook to fix her stroganoff. If I'm going to act as a buffer between you and your daughters, then I get the good stuff!"

"I'll tell her," he said, then surprised me with a hug. "You're one of my best friends, Lance. I don't tell you that enough. This scares the shit out of me, and I might lose, but I can't not try it. I think I've been preparing for this all my life."

I hugged him back and when we pulled apart, I saw the emotion in my oldest friend's face. "I love you too, brother, and you'll do great. We both know you're made for this. I'll see you Friday, and help you convince the girls to put their lives in the political blender, again. It's not like they don't love it too."

He laughed, because he knew as well as I did that both of his daughters were just like him.

As far as Melody was concerned, she, too, was made for this. The woman was smart, intense, and had run a couple of very large software companies, growing them to the point that they sold for millions. She seemed to flow through politics like a duck swims through water.

I didn't know whether I wanted to help with a campaign or not, but it'd be fun to watch them spread their political wings. I already knew all four of them would be amazing at it.

The week sped by, and although I made my announcement that I wouldn't be running for reelection, the news flashed for a moment, then disappeared. Luckily, my position as state attorney general didn't bring on the same level of coverage as some of the other elected officials.

On Friday night, I showed up at the governor's mansion with roses from my garden that I knew Melody loved. The intense smell followed me the entire way, reminding me of my visit to Grandma's. When I reached the door, I admired the architecture and beautiful gardens surrounding the property.

Kelsey met me at the door, smiling. "Uncle Lance," she said, and I cocked an eyebrow.

"You only call me that when you want something. What's up?" I asked, and she chuckled.

Seconds later, Mandie, her sister, walked in and smiled. "She wants you to talk Jennie into coming out for her birthday party next month. She thinks because they're both over eighteen now, it'll be more fun than just hanging out with little ol' underage me."

Kelsey shot her sister a look that almost had me choking on my tongue. I resisted the urge to laugh, and said, "Why don't you call and ask her yourself?"

Kelsey's mouth formed a small pout, which was honestly out of character. She was more firestorm than pouter. "It's weird, don't you think, throwing yourself a birthday party?" I was surprised she worried about appearances.

"Um, Kelsey, I'll ask, but when did you start worrying about what people think about you?"

She looked at me, concern showing on her face, but shook it off quick enough. "Never, it's just I think it'd keep it from being uncomfortable. Anyway, come on in. I think Dad's finishing some stuff up, and Mom's out in the garden."

Mandie came up behind her sister as she rushed off, taking the flowers. "So, what's really going on?" I asked, sure her sister would know and, of course, would tell on her.

Mandie looked shy. "Well, things might be changing, and appearances are gonna be more important maybe..."

I smiled. I knew these two had probably already picked up the situation enough to know what was happening. I also knew they hadn't been officially told yet.

I shrugged as she turned and followed her sister into the kitchen while I continued toward the back of the house to find Melody.

When I went out into the backyard, Melody was in the garden cutting flowers for, I assumed, a dining-room table centerpiece. She gathered up the bouquet and came over as soon as she noticed me. "It's been a while," she said, and I bowed at the chastisement.

"That it has. Sorry, but in my defense, work has been a little hectic lately."

"Okay, I'll forgive you, but only because you're here now and will help mitigate the storm that's brewing."

"Melody, you know they already know, right?"

She looked surprised. "Why? Did they say something?"

"Yep, your oldest met me at the door wanting me to invite my daughter to her birthday party, because if she invited Jennie herself, it might be... unseemly. Your youngest then mentioned keeping up appearances."

Melody twisted her elegant mouth in thought. "They have their radar honed like the Navy. How they've figured it out, I'll never know."

I chuckled. "Gerald has been a politician practically their whole lives..."

"They are smart, aren't they?"

"More than a little."

With that, Melody put her arm in mine and drew me into the house. "Dinner is going to be a little late. Gerald is dealing with some unsavory problems at the moment," she said, and led me into the living room and began arranging the cut flowers into an empty vase.

"Are those unsavory problems here at the residence?"

"Lance, you've always been a troublemaker." She laughed but didn't answer me. "Anyway, I've got a favor to ask."

I looked at the woman, sensing trouble. She only put her Southern First Lady airs on when she was up to something. More often than not, her *up to something* usually landed me in trouble. Melody was a master manipulator, and after many years of being friends, I knew the signs of being managed.

"Melody, I come in peace," I said.

She burst out laughing, and her pristine façade cracked a bit. "Okay, you know me too well, but I do have a huge favor."

I nodded, careful not to commit to anything until I had all the information.

"Well," she said quietly, I assumed to keep the conversation confidential. "There'll be a formal announcement, and we will be doing that at one of our biggest sponsor's homes."

My suspicions grew. I knew who their biggest donor was, which would certainly not bode well for me.

"It would mean the world to all of us if you were there when we made the announcement."

I shook my head. "I love you, Melody, but you know I don't get along with them. It's not in anyone's interest for us to be in the same part of the state, much less the same house."

"I know, and I wouldn't normally ask, but we need them."

"Sorry, that's a no for me. I'll be happy to throw my support behind you, but I'll not be going to my mom and grandparents' house. Not under any circumstances."

"Not even to help get Gerald the nomination?"

"Not even for that," I said. "Now, tell me about your trip to Stanford. Do you think Kelsey is going to get in?"

The abrupt change in subject was my way of saying I was done, and although I could tell she was having a difficult time letting the subject drop, she only hesitated a moment before the smile spread across her face.

"I think she'd be better off going to school close by. Oregon's got wonderful schools, but yeah, they seemed as interested in her as she was of them. So, has Jennie decided what to do now she's graduated from college?" she asked.

"Maybe, but you know that woman is as stubborn as her parents." I smiled, despite myself. "And, yes, I include myself in that statement. She's very busy doing an apprenticeship with a famous artist and intends to spend some time in Chemeketa with her friend Scarlett, then who knows what's next."

I heard footsteps behind me and turned just in time to see two state senators come down the stairs. They weren't in the mood to chat, and after a perfunctory greeting, they left.

"That went well," Gerald said in his sarcastic way.

I laughed. "Yep, same old same old then. You know," I said in a hushed voice, "it will be at least a hundred times worse in D.C. At least in Oregon, most of the citizens are supportive of your more progressive ways."

As the family settled around the table, the meal was brought out to us in a very formal style, which still made me chuckle. I doubted anyone on the planet ate so formally any longer.

When we'd all finished eating, Gerald and Melody joined hands and told the girls their news.

"Girls, we have something we need to speak with you about," he began.

Both young women turned toward their father, waiting for him to continue. "Your mother and I have decided we'd like to run for President of the United States. Of course, we need you to be on board with this decision. As you know, it will drastically change your lives whether I win or not."

Both girls were smiling, and Kelsey looked at her sister and nodded. "There are a couple things we need to negotiate before we commit."

I raised an eyebrow, amused by these two, but not really that surprised. They would make excellent politicians themselves someday.

Gerald shook his head. "Of course, I would expect nothing less, Kelsey. What are your terms?"

When they were done negotiating terms, which to be honest, I'd been in less-organized meetings with Fortune 500 CEOs, all four of them were smiling. "So, it's official?" I asked, wanting to ensure they were all on the same page.

Both Kelsey and Mandie nodded. "We knew you eventually would, Dad," Kelsey said. "We figured you'd go for it since your term is ending. It couldn't be a better time."

The four of them stood up and came together into a big hug. I darted into the kitchen then, and grabbed the cake the cook had made, lit the candles I'd asked her to put on it, so it felt more like a celebration, and brought it out to the table.

All four of them exclaimed when they saw the cake, and Gerald winked at me.

"So, if you all are insane enough to take this on, then we should celebrate in style."

"How did you arrange this?" Melody asked.

"I called Colette when you invited me to dinner. She agreed to have this ready in case it was a positive outcome."

I turned to Kelsey and winked, and she smiled back at me.

The rest of the evening was spent talking about the upcoming announcement. I darted away from questions that involved me going to my grandparents'. Melody was far from done with it, but I'd be damned and then damned again if I ever set foot on their property again.

The dreams began to torment me more and more as the nights went on. I suspected it was because Melody had asked me to go to my grandparents' house for the announcement.

When I'd moved to New York, I'd ceased all contact with them. Even when I came back to Oregon, I tried to keep my distance, despite navigating in the same political circles. Mom and Dad had divorced shortly after he kicked us out, but Mom hated my dad's mother with a passion, and therefore, considered us tainted since we'd moved in with her.

I hadn't spoken to my mom in all that time, even when we accidentally bumped into each other at my grandparents' estate. She pretended I was just one of their guests and smiled, nodded, and quickly disappeared.

That was my preference anyway. The woman no longer represented anything like a parent to me, and even though I suffered my grandparents for Gerald's sake, I drew the line at her.

I got the phone call from Gerald's campaign manager—yes, he'd gotten one of those fast enough—the next week. I was feeling bad, my throat had begun to hurt, and the dreams were taking over my sleep, making me toss and turn instead of getting any rest.

When he told me the only way my grandparents would agree to allow Gerald to use their home for his announcement was if I accompanied him, I flat-out refused. "I'm sorry, Gerald should pick a different place then. Maybe he should announce with a family that are actually loyal to the party."

I heard the man's gasp when I said that and immediately felt guilty. I'd need to be on the guy's good side if I intended to help Gerald's campaign.

"Sorry," I quickly added. "I'm feeling a bit under the weather, but no, I don't get along with my grandparents, and I'm not going to be manipulated into going to their home. They are anti-everything I stand for anyway, and I don't want to be associated with them."

I knew he was upset, but he was nice enough when he disconnected. I took the rest of the day off, and went home to get some rest, and hopefully kick whatever cold or flu I was developing.

Unfortunately, sleeping during the day didn't help any. The dreams of dark figures dancing around me continued, but now, images of my mom and grandparents mixed in with it.

I had my assistant drop off Theraflu and various other medications that did absolutely nothing to help, and over the next few days, things continued to get worse.

I finally gave up and went to the doctor, who did a million tests and said he knew what I didn't have, but there was no sign of what I did have.

I didn't have the flu, strep, or other common illnesses, but I had a combination of symptoms of several things.

He ended up recommending over-the-counter meds and to keep my fluids up. Oh, and if it got any worse, let him know.

I decided the best thing I could do, since I apparently wasn't contagious, was to keep working and hope I could close down my cases, or at least get them to the point I could hand them off to my deputy before the election. I stumbled into the office after the weekend, and although my staff gave me a wide berth, I managed to get some work done.

When Melody knocked on my door in the early afternoon, I didn't have the diplomacy to stifle my moan.

The woman looked me over and shook her head. "That's a horrible response to seeing me at your office, Lance," she said.

"I'm sorry, I'm not feeling well, and I know you're here to bully me into going to my grandparents."

She sat down across from me.

"Have you been to the doctor? You look awful."

"Thanks, Melody. Yes, I've been to the doctor, and I know I look pretty sick, but I don't seem to have anything medically wrong with me, at least nothing they can find. So, I'm stuck being sick without being sick..." I hesitated a moment, and added, "You know this all started when you mentioned my grandparents, it's possible that's what's behind all this."

She huffed. "Good try, but you've dealt with them before, and it didn't hurt you."

"Why are you picking on me, Melody?" I said in a pouty whine that was very unlike me, at least unlike the highly crafted persona I let others see.

She chuckled. "Well, I wouldn't do this if I didn't have to, but we need you, and we really need your grandparents. They represent the more conservative side of the party, the side we'll need if we're to compete with the more liberal elements. If we can campaign more toward the center, we have a better chance of winning the nomination as well as the general election."

"Why do they want me there?" I asked, resigned.

"They didn't say, but I'm guessing it's because they're getting older. Of your brothers, you've said yourself, you are more like them than the others. You're in politics, your brothers aren't. You're the oldest, so you know them better. Your grandmother is very ill, and your grandfather is in his eighties. Maybe they want to make up?" she said.

I laughed humorlessly. "That is highly unlikely. Besides, even if we reunited, I'm too old to chase after their money for campaign donations."

"I have a suggestion. I can ask if they'll make an exception if you can just meet before the party, have a discussion with them, then leave before the announcement, especially with you feeling ill, we can use that as a reason for your not being present."

I sighed deeply. "Melody, I'll meet with them if it's required, but I resent it, and it'll be one time, never again. You need to make sure they understand that. If they ask again, I'll simply refuse. You and Gerald need to know that as well. You can't ever ask me to do this again. It's a promise I'll require if I agree. I can't tell you how much I don't want to do this, and if we weren't so close, I frankly wouldn't even consider it."

I looked her in the eye and waited, determined to ensure she understood what it meant.

She looked sad. "I'm sorry to ask this of you, and we understand. We won't ask again. This will be the last time."

"Set up the meeting for before the party. I'll meet with them, then I'll go home, no questions asked. Oh, you should also warn them, if they try to manipulate me or trick me into staying, I will make a scene, and it won't be good for anyone if I do."

She nodded. I hoped she understood, I wouldn't be played. I figured she and Gerald were smart enough not to try. My mom and her parents, that was a different story.

Of course, this was all part of the reason why I had trust issues. I loved Gerald like a brother... maybe even more since I tended to avoid my brothers and never once had I avoided Gerald. But, politics didn't give a damn about you as a person. No one was above pushing their agenda when they wanted something and had the money to pursue it.

I didn't really blame them though, it was how you won elections. Now that I thought about it, I guessed I didn't really even mind going to my grandparents'. It was time to be done with them once and for all and this gave me the opportunity I needed to put an end to their meddling.

As far as Mom was concerned, well, she no longer fit that role anyway. After all these years of being estranged, it was time for me to let them all go, once and for all.

Seven

Drew

I HADN'T SEEN GWEN'S spirit since the night Lance had visited, and, of course, it worried me. I'd last seen her stand between her son's cantation and me, after all. That couldn't have boded well for her, especially since she existed in a dimension no longer her own.

My agent contacted me the day after the property had been cleansed. I'd usually take that as a sign of something good, as I tended to get important gigs after a big spell. However, I couldn't help but feel it was ominous. The fact it was a short-notice request made it even worse.

The governor had become a good customer of mine following my decision to mostly perform regionally. When Gwen had initially gotten sick, I decided I wanted to spend as much time with her as I could, so I cut back my touring schedule considerably. As a result, I tended to get booked throughout the Pacific Northwest, including several political functions in and around the state capital.

This latest gig was another such event. The governor's office sent a list of songs they wanted, and as always, they were the more classical. As a tenor, however, I'd come to expect it and was never surprised that the old arias tended to be requested more often than not.

The other song I tended to sing often for the governor was Sufjan Stevens's "City of Roses." I contacted my band, and when they all said they were available, I booked the engagement.

The band—Oliver, Lily, and Pete, all of whom I'd known since I'd been a young man—usually met at my place to practice, especially when the weather was nice. We practiced several of our songs, and as the evening progressed, Oliver pulled out his homebrew as we had a jam session out in the garden. When we were confident we were ready for the show, we all sat back and just enjoyed hanging out as friends.

Our soundcheck reverberated across the manicured lawn of the very large and pretentious home we were performing at this evening. Luckily, the way the house and yard were positioned with trees behind and beside us led to the acoustics being better than normal outside.

We had an hour before guests were supposed to arrive, and all of our equipment was set up and ready. Earlier in the day, the weather had looked bad when we left the coast, and I was concerned that we'd be stuck performing in a small indoor space, but luckily, Salem wasn't as prone to rainy weather as Chemeketa.

We'd just finished all the instrumental checks when I heard someone hacking up a lung. If we were in

Chemeketa, I'd have offered to help, since one of my abilities was to help people boost their immune systems, but here, away from my home, I was reticent to get too involved. Outside people were less open-minded to a witch's remedies.

Despite that, the hacking seemed to be out of control, so I fetched some homemade horehound cough drops out of my satchel and followed the sound.

I froze when I saw him. Lance Franklyn looked like death warmed over. His suit was pristine, of course, but he was pale, looked like he'd lost weight, and I could tell he felt awful.

He was talking to some older man, who appeared to be reaming him about something. Something told me to hold back a moment and wait. Within seconds, the confrontation was over, and the older man turned on his heels and stomped back up toward the house.

Lance turned and appeared to sway. I rushed toward him, wrapped my arms around him, and asked if he was okay.

He looked at me surprised, then reached into his coat pocket and pulled out a handkerchief. "I'm okay, just got a bad cold I can't seem to shake."

I nodded, knowing exactly what was going on, and handed him the two cough drops. "Here, take these. They'll help a little, but you know I did warn you."

He looked at me oddly, our faces only inches apart. "Drew," he began, then was hit with another coughing fit so I released my hold on him.

It was then that I saw the governor's wife come over. She looked concerned, but smiled at me nonetheless.

"Lance, are you okay? Honey, you look absolutely awful."

"Well, I'm still sick, and dealing with bigoted family members didn't help much. I'm going to go home and go to bed and toss and turn there."

Mrs. Mumford looked at me and smiled. "Hello, Drew. Are you ready for tonight?" she asked.

"Yep, we are. I heard Lance hacking, though, and came to check it out. Not that I knew it was him."

She looked at me curiously. "You know Lance?" she asked, but before I could answer he began coughing again.

"Yes, his grandmother, Gwen, was a friend of mine." I looked at the poor man and felt sorry for him. "I think we better help him get home. He looks dead on his feet."

She agreed, and we escorted him to a car sitting not far away.

"Jace, take Mr. Franklyn home," Mrs. Mumford told the waiting driver. "You can return for us after you drop him off."

"What about my car?" Lance asked.

"You are in no condition to drive. I'll have someone bring it to you," she said in a way that brokered no argument.

Lance shrugged, surrendering to her easier than I thought he would have if he hadn't felt so bad.

"So, how did it go?" she asked him, almost shyly.

"As you'd expect, they want me to denounce my sexuality and come be the heir apparent."

"Really? That's... shocking," she said.

"Yep, shocking..." Lance said sarcastically before coughing again.

When we tucked him into the car, he leaned over to me, and said, "If you know how to make this go away, I'm all ears."

"I'll drop your car off tomorrow morning, and we can talk then," I said quietly into his ear, then taking one of the horehound cough drops still clutched in his hand, I popped it into his mouth and shut the door.

We watched the car move down the long driveway and out the entrance. Mrs. Mumford looked back at me, and I could tell she wanted to ask questions.

"I'd better get back to the stage. The guests are already arriving."

She nodded, but the sly smile on her face definitely screamed caution to me. Damn, I'd seen that look enough on Gwen's face when she was playing matchmaker.

"Oh, Mrs. Mumford, I'm going to need someone to give the valet permission to give me Lance's keys, and I need his address too. We're staying at the Hilton tonight, and I'll take his car to him after I check out in the morning."

She nodded, the calculating look still on her face. I avoided any further discussion, however, by saying goodbye and darting off toward the stage.

EIGHT

— · —

LANCE

WHEN I'D ARRIVED AT my grandparents' house, their butler met me at the door and escorted me to my grandfather's office. My grandmother and mom were there as well.

I sat across the big desk in what I thought of as the interrogation chair. My mother sat in a wingback chair just out of sight, so if I wanted to look at her, I had to turn around. My grandmother sat cattycorner to my grandfather, so it was clear they were a unified force.

I sat in the chair and resisted the urge to cough. It was almost like a stand-off between them and me. After several long seconds, though, I looked at my watch and said, "You're on a very tight schedule here. I've only agreed to be here for a few minutes, so if you've got a reason for summoning me and using my friends to force my presence, I'd suggest you get to it."

My grandmother's face darkened. She was always the one who said we should respect our elders, and even if we'd never had our falling out, I doubted she'd ever see me as anything more than a snot-nosed kid. Regardless, she didn't remark, which, to be honest, was something different.

"You are the heir to our estate," my grandfather said. "You need to take responsibility now, while we are still around."

"I'm not sure why you want me to be your heir. You've made it clear my entire adult life that you think we are trash. You've alienated my brothers and me for practically our whole lives, so I simply can't understand why you even consider us your family."

He cleared his throat, and putting on his CEO voice, said, "We do not and never will agree to your lifestyle choices, however, you are the eldest grandson and, besides your brothers, our only logical heir. Your grandmother is sick, I'm old, and your mother isn't..." He looked over at her, then back at me. "She has declined the position of heir."

That shocked me. I'd admit I didn't know much about my mother, not since that night when my father went nuts and cursed us. I couldn't imagine she'd pass up the opportunity to run a multimillion-dollar company, though.

I took a deep breath and, after breaking into a long coughing fit, got myself together enough, to say, "I'm not your heir. I'm sorry, I know you want me and my brothers to be something we aren't. If you'd wanted to be a part of our lives, then you should've made the effort long ago. I don't need your money or your home. I don't want to be the CEO of your grocery-store chain either." I thought for a moment before I continued, deciding to make my feelings crystal clear. "I'm a gay man, I'm never going to be straight. The world knows I'm a gay man, and pretending I'm not wouldn't serve me, especially in exchange for your money. As far as Mom is concerned, she couldn't care less whether we're alive or dead. I'm not even sure why she's here now, except maybe to try to entice me into wanting a relationship with her. Unfortunately, that ship has also sailed. As an attorney, my recommendation is that you liquidate the company, sell it, or better yet, make it an employee-owned enterprise. Do what you wish with it, with your estate. None of us expected to ever receive anything from you anyway, nor do we want it."

I stood to go, but began coughing again and almost doubled over, but not one of them moved to help me. That, if anything, showed just exactly who these people really were.

When I'd caught my breath, I cleared my throat, and said, "I suspect this is the last time I'll see you or speak to you, so let me say this too. I don't approve of your lifestyle either. You pretend to be something you aren't. You sit here in this enormous mansion on these extensive grounds and pass judgment on the people around you. You throw your money around as a way to force people to comply with your demands, including using it to get Gerald to force me here today. I have no respect for someone who lives like that. I've worked for presidents, governors, huge corporations, and I'm currently working for the great state of Oregon. Yet you still treat me as if I'm less than you. So, you may not approve of my lifestyle, whatever that means, but you should know that feeling is mutual."

I didn't wait for a response. Instead, I left the office and walked toward the area where Gerald and Melody told me they'd be. I wanted them to know I'd fulfilled my obligations. Unfortunately, I'd only reached the backyard when my grandfather came up behind me. Had I not been sick, I think I could've avoided him, but he cornered me up against the stage and began yelling.

"You're an ungrateful faggot who's never valued your birthrights or privileges."

I put my hand up, and said, "You are a rich, old bigot who's never had anyone point out how entitled he is." I so wanted to rant more, but just then a coughing fit came on me even worse than before. Sweat popped out across my forehead, and I felt as if I was going to pass out.

Unfortunately, when I managed to get myself together, the old man was still standing there, his entitled ass waiting for me to finish coughing, so he could continue berating me.

"You want to blame us for not being a family, for ignoring you and your brothers, but that blame is squarely on your shoulders. We are your elders, we are the ones who deserve respect, and any decent person would know that."

The coughing came on me again, preventing me from responding , but as the cough subsided this time, so did my anger. When I stood up and looked at him again, I simply said, "We aren't anything to each other. You should stop trying for all our sakes."

He turned then and walked away, and I turned to leave. Part of me knew this was the final time I'd have to deal with them. *Again*, I thought, *it's no wonder I have such trust issues...*

For a moment, dizziness overwhelmed me, and I thought I might fall, but that was when a mirage showed up and wrapped me in his arms. "Drew?" I asked, just before another coughing fit took me.

Damn, is this getting worse? How is it getting worse?

Drew asked me if I was okay, and realizing he was indeed real, I nodded. I felt too vulnerable at that moment, not so much from the confrontation with my grandparents since nothing said tonight hadn't been said before, but because I was so sick. I just felt like an open wound smeared in salt.

Melody came over then, and the two of them loaded me into Melody and Gerald's car and sent me home. I was so sick I couldn't even get myself to worry about my vehicle. When Drew said he'd bring it by, I left with no more complaints.

I spit out the nasty tasting cough drop Drew shoved in my mouth and stuck it in the small trash can that sat between the seats. I ended up falling asleep in the back seat and found myself floating around in the same old dreams I'd been having since I'd become sick. Images of dark smoke gagged me when I inhaled it. Dark creatures, mostly wolves, but sometimes snakes and others, snapped at me.

Occasionally, I'd see the image of my father or hear his voice, laughing or taunting me.

Sometimes, I'd catch a glimpse of my grandma, but it was as if she couldn't get to me, as if I were in the mouth of a cave, and all she could do was look in at me.

I woke up in my bed, unsure how I'd gotten there. My shoes were off, and my suit jacket lay over my bedroom chair, otherwise, I was still completely dressed.

I was too weak to get up, though, so I only managed to roll over before drifting back to sleep.

The dreams became more intense, more maniacal. My father's figure was no longer just a dark shape. I could make out his features, although they were shaded. He loomed over me, prodding me with something sharp, and laughing.

When I looked down, I could see welts coming up wherever he stabbed me, but I was too weak, too sick to do anything about it. It was then I knew I was going to die, and to be honest, besides my daughter Jennie, I had no real reason to live, so I closed my eyes and drifted away, until something shifted for me, and my father's figure disappeared. The nightmare subsided, and I was drifting in an uneasy peace.

I knew it meant I was in my final stages of life, and I was okay with that. My only regret was that I couldn't say goodbye to Jennie and that I'd never found love. I'd only had the remnants of love, but nothing real, no one who loved me.

I thought of my brothers, Kyle and Crea, and felt the tears run down my cheek. No, I had them. We loved each other, despite coming from a family incapable of loving one another. That was a real blessing.

With that thought, I drifted away into darkness and blessed oblivion.

NINE

DREW

THE CONCERT WENT WONDERFULLY. We ended our set with "City of Roses", and the governor and his family took our place on the stage to a standing ovation.

"I would like to thank the band for their incredible performance tonight and for all of you who came to celebrate with us."

The crowd cheered, and even though we were in the back yard of a large mansion, for a moment, it almost felt like a big concert instead of a formal event.

"We are celebrating something big tonight," he continued when the cheering died down. "My family have served the incredible state of Oregon for more than a decade. We've been honored and humbled by this wonderful opportunity."

A hush fell over the crowd, anticipation growing, and I could tell there were questions about whether this was the end, or the beginning of something.

"We believe in the democracy of this great nation, and we believe for that democracy to survive in modern times, there must be people who stand up for it, make sacrifices for it, and do what is necessary to help it to thrive. Mandie, Kelsey, Melody, and I have decided to step up to the plate and offer ourselves to the service of this nation. In the words of a great man and leader of our country, John Kennedy, 'Ask not what this country can do for you, ask what you can do for your country.' We hear that call tonight, and therefore, we are announcing our bid for our party's nomination for President of the United States."

The crowd screamed and cheered for what felt like a full minute.

I'd thought it strange that we'd been asked to play "God Bless America," but now it made sense. We came back out on stage and ended the evening with that song, everyone in the crowd singing with us. It was an emotional experience and one that would go down in the books as something I'd remember for the rest of my life. Whether the governor won the nomination, or the election was irrelevant, the spirit of the evening was such that I knew something big was happening, something important was afoot, and my little band and I had been a part of it.

The rest of the night was a full-out party. The band and I were officially done with our set, so we wandered around, shaking hands, and celebrating with the crowd.

After the party broke up, we packed our gear and instruments into the van. I sent the others on, telling them I'd agreed to drive a friend's car home and would meet them back at the hotel.

Luckily, I was able to retrieved the keys with no difficulty from the valet, who also handed me a sealed envelope with Lance's address in it.

The moment I touched the envelope, I felt the panic. Gwen's panic. It was well after midnight, but I knew I had to reach Lance now. He couldn't wait until morning.

I loaded Lance's address into my phone's GPS and let it lead me to his house. The moment I started along the highway, I saw in my periphery the dark mist I'd seen in my dream quest. The monster was on the move, and I was its target.

Luckily, I was still protected. I'd had a couple of drops of Gwen's potion in my tea or coffee every morning, and I'd worn a couple of protections in the form of medicine bags and kept an amulet I'd inherited from *my* grandmother in my satchel. So, I knew I was mostly safe from the darkness. Lance, I was certain, wasn't.

I was surprised to find he lived in a nice two-story home, surrounded by what I thought might be gardens, but the dark prevented me from seeing them clearly.

I dashed up to the door, found a doorbell and rang it. I knocked as well, but I knew deep inside he wouldn't answer.

"Gwen, if you're here, I need your help!"

"Go to him..." I heard a whisper, and knew it was her.

I looked at the car keys, found the one I thought was probably his house key, and shoved it in the lock.

I walked into the house and was immediately thrown back. The mist swirled around the interior, filling every corner. I coughed when it encircled me, but I stood up to it and sang a Gregorian chant-style prayer.

"Great Mother, hear my prayer,
Wash off the evil to find the path,
Lead me onto roads so clear,
Banish darkness from this seer."

When the darkness began to clear, I walked forward, lifting my voice, and singing the same verse over and over, letting the light of the moon seep into me as I went.

By the time I got to the stairs, the dark had retreated to the corners, but the malice was still strong.

I rushed up the stairs singing the chant until I made it to where I intuitively knew Lance slept. When I entered the room, the cantation stood over him, and a dark web-like substance seemed to emanate from Lance's body, flowing into the cantation.

"Stop!" I yelled. The cantation didn't even turn toward me. I could tell Lance was completely engulfed in its grip. I had to stop this somehow, but my mind was blank. I turned to look around the room for anything that might help, and my eyes settled on Gwen's potion. Lance had placed it on his dresser.

I found a glass half full of water, poured several drops into the glass, and drew the mixture into my mouth before spewing it all over the cantation.

It shrieked, unlike any cantation I'd ever seen or heard before. This one had begun to take form.

"From the potion of thy mother, I cast you out of this home!"

I took another mouthful and spewed it onto the cantation again, then repeated my chant.

"From the potion of thy mother, I cast you out of this home!"

The cantation spun toward me then and raised clawed hands, and just like in the dream quest, it rushed me. I took the rest of the water in my mouth, and as the cantation came within reach, I spat it all into its face.

It spun away, melting into the black mist, not unlike the Wicked Witch of the West had done in *The Wizard of Oz*, and I continued to chant.

"From the potion of thy mother, I cast you out of this home!"

As I chanted, the air cleared, and when I was confident the entity was gone, I rushed back to Lance's car, pulled out my satchel, and lit a sage bundle I'd brought with me.

I walked around his extremely large home, making sure to fill every corner, every crevice, with smoke from the sage while chanting my favorite cleansing chant. The house was so large it took me almost an entire hour to cleanse the interior. I figured I could cleanse the outside the following day.

I was exhausted from the concert, casting out the dark entity, and doing the cleansing, but now that the place was safe, I could check on Lance.

I went back up to his bedroom, afraid of what I'd find. Lance was stone cold, but still breathing. Tears and snot ran down his pale face, and I put the sage in a bowl on his nightstand so he could inhale the smoke.

In his ensuite, I found a small container and a wash-cloth. I also refilled his glass with water and put some of Gwen's potion in each.

I wiped down his face and chest, and anywhere his skin was exposed, then I lifted him up gently and en-couraged him to drink some of the water. At first he didn't respond, but I whispered the song I'd sung tonight, "City of Roses." It was a beautiful song and resonated with me.

As I sang, Lance began to stir, and I managed to get him to take a few sips. Almost instantly, his rigid body began to relax.

"That's enough for now," I said, somehow knowing he was past the point of concern. I went back into his ensuite and washed my own face.

When I came back out, he was sound asleep. I sat next to him, placing my hand over his third eye, and I could tell the dreams were natural, nothing was there interrupting or infecting them.

I went over to a nice recliner in the corner of the room, picked his suit jacket up and hung it in the closet, then kicked my shoes off and lay back in the recliner for what I hoped was a couple hours rest myself.

TEN

LANCE

I WOKE UP ACHING all over. Like having the flu but several times worse. My room smelled of smoke, like when my grandmother cleansed her home, and I sat up looking for her. Of course, she wasn't there, but sitting in my bedroom recliner was... Drew?

Groaning, I got up and was about to head over to wake him when I had a sudden urge to pee.

When I came back into the room, the man was still out.

I had no idea why he was in my house, or for that matter, my bedroom, but memories of last night made me think maybe he had saved me. Of course, I was probably going as insane as everyone else in my grandmother's community, so I just shrugged and crawled back into bed.

My glass of water from a couple nights ago was sitting on my nightstand and feeling dreadfully thirsty, I chugged it and almost choked when it tasted like my grandmother's tea.

When did I make that? Then, I looked at Drew and remembered him propping me up to drink it last night.

The memory was vague and felt more like a dream than reality.

As the still-cool liquid settled in my stomach, I began to feel better almost immediately. Not well, by any means—I was still achy and wanted to fall back to sleep—but I was better.

I laid my head back down, and sleep gently overtook me again. It seemed strange to sleep with him in my bedroom, but my body needed sleep more than it needed to kick the man out of the house.

When I woke later, he was gone.

Most of my achiness was gone as well, so I got out of bed, and noticing I'd slept in my suit, I cringed. I felt grimy and decided to take a shower.

When I'd finished, I wrapped the towel around my waist and walked into my bedroom, and came face to face with Drew Andreassen.

"Um, sorry, I thought you were still asleep," he said, blushing as his eyes crawled slowly up my bare torso.

I'd lost weight while I was sick, but despite that, I'd stayed in pretty decent shape. I worked out every morning at least, and most evenings, I did yoga before going to bed. I'd seen too many men who led similarly stressful lives let their bodies go to hell as they got older.

I wasn't particularly vain, but I didn't really want to be going around complaining about all my body parts falling apart either. I hoped a good exercise regimen would help me keep age away... at least as long as humanly possible.

When Drew's eyes finally settled on mine, they were full of shadows and sexual heat. The look immediately made my cock twitch. I'd already noticed the man was beautiful, with a sexy, slim build, and age had settled nicely along his facial features, making him look stronger, purer than he probably had as a younger man.

He cleared his throat, and the sexual haze disappeared from his expression.

"So, I see you're feeling better, that's good. I found some breakfast fixings in the kitchen and made you some food that should help your recovery as well." Then, he turned on his heels and headed out the door.

"Wait, Drew, why are you here?" I asked, but he was gone. I knew he'd probably heard me, but if he did, he didn't return.

The look of heat I'd seen on my houseguest's face made me hope, maybe in a pervy way, that he'd come back in, and we'd get to explore some of the unspoken options his expression promised. Instead, once again alone in my bedroom, I finished getting ready.

As I came down the stairs a few minutes later, I was immediately confronted with the smell of bacon frying. My house hadn't smelled so good in some time, and I hadn't bought bacon, or had I? I tended to eat out or have food delivered at the office and rarely used the kitchen.

Drew smiled when he saw me. "You're looking much better," he said before turning back to the stove.

"I *am* better," I said hesitantly, causing him to turn back to me. His gaze lingered on my face a moment before taking the bacon off the stove and placing it on a paper towel. He poured the oil out of the pan, wiped it down, and cracked three eggs into it. Covering it, he turned the stove off, checked his watch, and came over to me.

"So, you're wondering why I'm here, I'm guessing."

I nodded, sure the confusion showed on my face.

"What do you remember?" he asked.

"I remember leaving you at the party, which... why were you at the party?"

"I was the entertainment. I'm in a band."

Instantly, I remembered the band Melody liked for her formal events. I hadn't put two and two together until then.

"That's you? I've seen you perform then. How didn't I put that together?"

Drew laughed. "I'm guessing you saw me as the guy who lived with your grandmother, not someone cool enough to sing with a band."

He continued smiling when he looked at his watch and went to check on the eggs. Satisfied, he lifted the lid and slipped one of the eggs into a bowl. "Do you like your eggs runny?" he asked.

"Where did you get eggs and bacon?" I asked.

He plated the food and brought it over to me. "The eggs were in the refrigerator, and luckily weren't out of date yet. The bacon I found in your freezer."

He sat across from me and began to mix his egg into what appeared to be oatmeal. "Um, is that oatmeal?" I asked, scrunching up my face.

He laughed at my expression. "I actually brought this with me, it's organic. I usually only eat naturally farmed eggs, but beggars can't be choosers."

"You brought your own oatmeal? Are you on a diet or something?" I asked while studying his body, which seemed perfect to me, no need for a diet.

"No, I'm mostly vegetarian. As a practitioner, I don't eat meat very often as it causes my energy to flow differently. I want to keep it pure."

I nodded, but didn't really understand.

I stuck a piece of bacon in my mouth and moaned. "Mmm, this is good. I'm glad I had it in the freezer."

Drew smiled, but prompted, "What else do you remember?"

"I remember waking up in the night, the coughing was worse, and I felt like I had a severe case of the flu. I fell back to sleep, but the dreams were really awful, like when you've been given a sedative you don't react well to."

"Tell me what happened at the end of your dream? Did you see anyone in particular?"

"At one point, I thought I saw my grandmother looking at me like I was in a cave, but she couldn't get to me. She looked really sad and concerned. After that, it felt like I was dying, then I remember the nightmare seemed to settle, and I drifted into oblivion."

The thought of the dream unsettled me, and I lost my appetite.

Drew looked at me for a long time, before responding, "I believe in being honest with someone, even when they're skeptical, or when they don't understand how the universe works regarding what you'd call magical energies. I know that's going to upset you, but I'd rather you be upset by the truth than lie and let things get bad again." He paused, clearly trying to choose his words carefully. "The day you left Chemeketa, I went to see a hedge witch. They have very honed skills with divination and understanding obstacles we're up against.

Long story short, I went on what's called a dream quest, or a vision quest, with her and was attacked by something dark and foreboding. We call it a cantation, as I've told you before, that's a physical representation of a cast spell. They're often negative and appear when dark spells have been cast. In this case, it was a cantation of your father. I've already told you your grandmother is still speaking with me, and she was there in my dream quest. She even protected me, but not before the cantation physically attacked me. If it hadn't been for some fast work on the part of the hedge witch and her daughter who has healing skills, I'm guessing my life would've ended."

I stared at him for a long time, slowly digesting not only his story, but what it all might mean for him and me. I hadn't told him I'd seen my father, who wasn't my father, in my dreams throughout the past few weeks. It sounded a lot like what he was saying he'd experienced.

"Last night before the party, I heard you coughing. I didn't know it was you, but I knew whoever it was had a serious illness that I hoped to relieve some with my homemade horehound drops. Then I saw it was you, and knew it was worse than that. As I had warned you before you left my home, the darkness that had haunted me was causing you to be sick."

I shook my head. "No, I had a bad cold."

He chuckled. "Did you go to a doctor?" he asked, and I nodded. "And what was the doctor's diagnosis?"

I hesitated. The doctors hadn't been able to diagnose it at all.

He saw my hesitation and, ignoring my skepticism, continued, "The moment I got your car keys in my hand,

I knew you were in trouble. I came right over, and was confronted by the same black mist from the dream I had when you spent the night. It was also the same mist from my dream quest when I was attacked. That, however, was in this dimension, which is really scary, Lance. When things progress so far that they exist in this realm, they are beyond dangerous."

He paused, allowing the impact to settle in, though I was still struggling to wrap my head around all of it.

He looked down at his oatmeal and then back up at me. "I managed to clear a path and made it to your bedroom. The cantation was standing over you, drawing your life force into itself. You were comatose at that point and very close to death." Drew took in a long breath and let it out slowly, like he was still processing all of this himself. "If it hadn't been for your grandmother's potion and the fact that you'd put it within reach, I'm not sure I could've stopped it from killing you. After I managed to get it away from you, it got very angry and attacked me again. If the dream quest was any indication, it would've killed me."

Drew looked down at his hands again. I could tell he was getting his wits about him, but it sounded so farfetched. I'd struggled with my grandmother's religion. People dancing around under the moon, chanting silly rhymes, I just couldn't digest it was real.

Drew seemed to sense my reticence, and when he looked back up at me, his face was expressionless.

"I-I don't know what to say," I said, and he nodded.

"I understand, Lance. I knew you were a skeptic before we met, but your life is in jeopardy and so is mine. Somehow that thing has gotten stronger, and I suspect it has something to do with whoever you were arguing with last night. Even if you don't trust me or what I'm telling you, you're likely to end up in the same situation as last night, or worse. Once the entity can get to you, once it's found its way into this dimension, it'll come easier next time. Do you have anything of your grandmother's that could help keep you safe? Did she leave you anything in the chest she'd kept for you?"

I nodded. "Yeah, I have a ring, one she'd had made from parts of her wedding ring."

"That's perfect," Drew said. "Wear it or put it in a bag and keep it in your pocket. I was able to chase the entity off this time, but I had to use Gwen's energy. A mother's energy is powerful regarding her children. Since it was your father who cast the curse, it is vulnerable to Gwen's potion, but I also guess her loving you so much and wanting to protect you has some bearing on it as well. I'm going to go, but before I do, I want you to understand, skeptic or not, this isn't an illusion. It isn't something you can hide from. Your father cast a vicious spell against you, and if you ignore it again, you *will* become its victim."

His words shocked me into silence. I honestly didn't know which was crazier or scarier at this point, believing him or not, so I just sat rooted to my chair. Drew hesitated a moment, before he continued, "I loved your grandmother, but I'm not going to chase you around trying to protect you, that's not my job. If you decide you want help, find me and I'll do what I can. Until then, use one or two drops of your grandmother's potion every morning. I use it in my tea or coffee. Wear the ring your grandmother left you, since that's a powerful tool for protection. If the sickness continues, call me."

He looked at his watch and walked toward the living room. He picked up what appeared to be his satchel, and said, "Eat your breakfast, you'll need the strength. Your body's been through some massive trauma these past few weeks, Lance."

He looked at me for a moment as if he wanted to say more, but sadness filled his face. "I wish I could do more for you, Lance..." He stopped himself then and turned, opened my front door, and walked out.

I stared at the food for a long moment and got up to go see if he was planning on walking home. Instead, I saw a car pulling away down my drive. He must have called for a Lyft or Uber before I came down, considering it usually took forty-five minutes for someone to get this far out.

I felt like an ass. Why did the man always make me feel like that? Like I was somehow lacking, because I didn't trust him or his hocus pocus.

I closed the door, found my keys sitting next to it on the table where I always left them, and smiled. He somehow knew that. He also knew I'd gotten worse when I'd spoken to my mother's family. I was a diehard skeptic, and if I was being honest, it was probably because I didn't want to believe my father had the ability to keep me and my brothers from ever finding love.

However, it was becoming more and more difficult to deny the facts, especially since after Drew had appeared last night, all the symptoms that had plagued me for weeks had vanished. I'd gone from possible hospitalization to feeling a little achy and tired.

I went back to the kitchen, finished eating the bacon and eggs he'd made me, then took the dishes, including his uneaten oatmeal, and placed it all in the sink. I was too tired to clean the kitchen, so I went back upstairs and crawled into bed.

I glanced around the room and saw the bottle of my grandmother's potion on my dresser. With Drew's warnings still fresh in my mind, despite my skepticism, I decided better safe than sorry and fetched the bottle. I let a couple drops fall on my tongue, moaned because it tasted nasty in its concentrated form and quickly washed it down with what little water was left in my glass, and lay down for another bout of sleep.

As soon as my head hit the pillow, I was transported to Grandma's house.

There were flowers everywhere, almost like a cartoon version of her gardens. I looked over to where an old fir tree used to stand, but had long-ago been cut down. We used to have a swing in that tree, and I saw my grandmother sitting there.

I ran over to her and sat on the grass like I'd done when I was little. Sometimes she'd read us a book while she sat in the old swing, and although I hadn't thought of it in years, it was a warm and happy memory.

Grandma looked sternly at me. "You're going to have to stop being so fucking stubborn, Lance," she said. "It might hurt your feelings, but, son, you are more like your father than both your brothers combined. You can't ignore your gifts just because you don't like what happened, or what you dished back at him in return. I'm not going to sit by and watch you die, and damn it, Lance,

I almost saw that last night. There was nothing I could do, you were lost to me. If it hadn't been for Drew..."

A tear slid down her cheek, and I sighed. "Grandma, I don't want to think about it. I don't want him to have that kind of power against me, against us."

She regarded me a long moment and then nodded. "And that's it, isn't it? That's why you work so hard not to believe." She chuckled but it was humorless. "In some ways, you're more superstitious than anyone in Chemeketa, thinking you can wish the gift away."

I could feel her love and concern for me, along with a steely resolve I'd always admired about the woman. I'd always thought I'd inherited that quality from her, though I felt far from strong or determined right now.

"Go to Drew. You are going to have to trust him. Trust yourself and your abilities. Drew's part of your destiny and the path to overcoming your father. Like it or not, and probably because of me, the two of you are linked on this quest. Your dad's spirit is too strong, too willful, to defeat alone. He will stop at nothing, I'm afraid, not even sparing your life in achieving his goal."

I felt like crying. "Grandma, why does he hate us so much?"

She shook her head, her expression one of deep pain. "He doesn't hate you, he wants to control you, there's a difference. I haven't been able to connect with him physically or spiritually in a long time, so I don't know what's causing this level of anger against you, but I do know you can't let it continue. You need to go to Drew and let him help you resolve this once and for all."

I stood up, and my tiny grandmother came and pulled me into a hug. "Is he really seeing you?" I asked, and she chuckled for real this time.

"Of course, he was my best friend... my twin flame in many ways. I can't leave until this is resolved, not just for you but for all my grandsons. Luckily, Drew has a strong ability to see beyond into the hinterland, between this world and the next, so we can communicate fairly freely."

"Okay, Grandma, I'll go to him, but I'm not committing to all your witchy ways," I said, and didn't miss the gleam in her eyes at my words.

"You mean you ain't gonna go dancing under the moon in a field in the middle of Kansas?"

"That's a definite no," I said, and felt my grandmother's warm embrace and chuckle as I woke up.

The tears flowed then. I'd missed so much in all the years I'd spent avoiding her. She was my person, always had been, even when I was little, and my cold mother refused to show me any affection. Grandma would scoop me up into her arms, hug me tight, and tell me how much she adored me. I had known complete acceptance and radiant, unconditional love in this life, and I owed it to my grandmother and myself to fight for it again.

ELEVEN

DREW

I WAS SO WORN out after leaving Lance's place, I slept in the back seat of the van all the way back to the Chemeketa. My bandmates all snuck glances at me the whole drive home, surely holding back a barrage of questions about where I'd disappeared to.

Their barely contained curiosity made me laugh. "You guys are funny," I said. "I spent the night nursing Gwen's grandson back to health after he almost collapsed at the party."

"Really, you're speaking to Gwen's grandchildren now?" Lily asked, surprised. They'd all heard me rant about how irresponsible and useless the three men were, perhaps slightly too often in retrospect.

"Yep, not that I really wanted to, but I got a feeling if I didn't the poor guy wouldn't have lasted the night."

All my bandmates knew my faith, and had experienced some pretty out-there things when someone had been injured or we were dealing with a nasty client. I even had them help me a few times when I needed to shift the energies toward the positive. I hadn't really discussed details, though, no need to scare them away, and I certainly didn't want to tell them some nasty entity related to a curse was out to get me.

"Is he at least good-looking?" Pete asked.

I rolled my eyes but couldn't deny it either. "He's really hot, but as the state's attorney general, he can be a bit stiff, and not in a good way," I said, which caused Lily to belt out a laugh.

I couldn't help but chuckle at the memories of my wilder younger days. Men came in and out of my life back then, like a revolving door, and I'd been more at home on the road touring than in any one place. I'd never have imagined myself putting down roots in a small town, let alone living in an old farmhouse with a woman more than twice my age who'd become my best friend.

Before I'd met Gwen, before I'd understood my gifts, I'd been a bit self-destructive. Of course, growing up with an abusive father certainly played into that. I was placed in foster care several times during my childhood. Somehow, I always seemed to be given back to my parents. My father would claim to have 'seen the light,' promised he was no longer using drugs, or that he'd given up alcohol, but it was all for show.

I moved out when I was sixteen and moved in with a friend who'd been adopted by my former foster parents. When I told them my father was still beating on me, they agreed to stretch the rules, let me move in, and pretended they were still my foster parents until I graduated.

Three days after my eighteenth birthday, probably because he no longer had me to beat on, my father shot my mother, then turned the gun on himself.

Even today, the feeling of loss wasn't really there. He'd beaten the love out of me, and my mom had always been unwilling to admit his abusive nature to the authorities. I'd learned long ago you didn't necessarily find love with the family you were born into. Family was something you created, not necessarily a product of genetics.

I guessed the thoughts were so fresh in my mind, because I was dealing with the reaction to the abusive nature of Lance's father. Luckily, mine never had the ability or knowledge of how to use energy, or else I was sure he'd have made my life even worse.

I felt so drawn to Lance, both emotionally and sexually. I'd wanted to hold him, comfort him when I saw him so vulnerable, and when he came out of the shower with only a towel wrapped around him, I'd wanted to do a whole lot more.

I think my heart went out to him more, because of the mutual understanding of how family could screw you up. Unlike Lance, however, I didn't have a Gwen in my life. Well, at least until I did. The moment I met her at the campgrounds in rural Eastern Kansas, I knew I'd found my home. It wasn't a place, it was a person.

I leaned up as we came over the mountains on the way back into Chemeketa. Pete was driving, and Lily and her husband, Oliver, were cuddled up asleep behind him. I crawled around the middle seat and sat in the front next to Pete.

"Hey, you finally wake up?" he asked.

"Sort of. I think I'll still sleep like the dead tonight. Remember when we could stay up all night and perform the next day?" I asked.

"Some of us still can."

I laughed. "You're still the baby of the group, so if any of us can, it would be you."

When we pulled into my driveway, I hugged everyone goodbye, then went into the house, and without unpacking anything, got ready to go to back to sleep.

I crawled into bed, passed out, and fell into a blissful dream of a certain attorney wrapped in my arms.

I hadn't had a wet dream since my twenties, but here I was, having one involving Lance Franklyn. I wondered what that meant. Maybe nothing, just the result of all the emotions stirred up dealing with his father, having my life threatened by that thing again, and seeing his very toned body freshly out of the shower.

One thing was for certain, it had been too long since I'd had a sexual relationship with someone. This was the longest I'd gone without at least a hookup, stretching back to before Gwen had gotten sick.

I got up the next morning resolved to let the universe fill that void, evil spirits and murderous cantations be damned. I needed to get laid.

Twelve

Lance

THE NEXT TWO WEEKS were all about handing my responsibilities over to my staff. I needed to begin preparing them for my departure, given the election was just a little over a year away. As the election drew nearer, I knew I'd be needed more and more here at the office, so if I were going to get away for an extended period, it was now or wait until the election.

I hardly ever took time off while being attorney general. For the most part, I loved having a full work life, because then I was never lonely, and I didn't have to face the depressing prospect of never finding love.

I closed up the house, gave the key to the groundskeeper, and headed west. This time I managed to let Drew know I was coming. I'd decided to stay in a small cottage outside of town and less than a mile from his property, knowing I would need to have my own space. However, I also knew I needed to connect with the man and get to know him better, maybe even develop a friendship. If my dreams were correct, and I'd had several since that first night I'd seen my grandmother, I needed to be in Chemeketa.

Drew had sounded hesitant when I announced I was coming, but he also sounded relieved when I told him I'd be staying in a cottage away from the farm. I tried not to take that too personally, not that I could blame him.

I texted my brother Crea, knowing since he was living there, I'd be in deep shit if I didn't at least try to contact him.

Hey, brother. I'm headed to Che. You there?

A few moments later, he texted back.

Nope, my new man and I are in Toronto. He's got a commission he's considering. I'm being wined and dined. You know, I can so get used to this.

I chuckled. My little brother wasn't someone I saw as uppity enough to want to be wined or dined, but hey, if he was happy... that was something. Encouraging even.

Fall was unleashing its usual vengeance on the coast as I pulled up to the little cottage. The rain drenched me as soon as I stepped out of my car, and I rushed to unload at least some of my luggage.

The evening, I sat back and just enjoyed the sound and smell of the rain that was just as much a part of my childhood memories as anything else. I was just about to drift off when my phone pinged.

It was a text from Drew.

What's your breakfast plans tomorrow morning?

I smiled, remembering the food he'd made for me at my house. Only then did it hit me that he'd cooked me bacon, despite not eating meat himself. Had my ex-husband ever been that thoughtful? Not even by half.

Nothing, I need to go shopping before I can cook here.

His reply came almost instantly, like he'd been waiting for my text.

Cool, when do you usually get up?

I laughed at that. I was an early riser, even as a kid.

Five usually.

Okay, that's too early for me, but Amelia's Restaurant downtown opens at nine. Meet you there?

I texted back a smiley face and a thumbs up.

See you then, was his final text.

I couldn't explain the uplift I felt in my heart with that silly text exchange. I almost felt like a teenager again, going on my first date.

I decided not to put too much weight on it, though. Best not to think too much, just let myself feel what I was feeling and deal with the ramifications later. If life had taught me one thing, it was that emotions weren't controllable, just how we reacted to them.

That night, I lay staring up at the ceiling of the little bedroom. I thought of all the things I'd avoided over the years. My grandmother, to some extent my brothers, definitely this little town. I felt sad, but actually, the real feeling was closer to ashamed.

I'd allowed my hateful parents to control my every move all the time, all the while thinking I'd been preventing that from happening. I realized I couldn't really blame them any longer; yes, they were horrible parents, but they hadn't kept me from the things and people I loved. I'd done that all on my own.

The next morning, I got up at my regular time, got dressed, and jogged down to the beach. The drizzle hadn't let up, but I loved how the mist hung over the water and the mountains that met the water at the shore. I'd always loved this beach as a child, and now, as an adult, I let myself enjoy my morning jog and the cold sprinkles that dripped down my face. It was exhilarating.

I jogged back up toward the cottage and passed the driveway that went up to Drew's. Before I could think, I turned and began jogging up to his house.

"Hello, Drew, are you up?" I yelled.

A few moments later, a sleep-rumpled, and extremely handsome Drew opened the front door. "What's up?" he asked. "I thought I was going to meet you... a little later."

I laughed. "Yeah, but I went for a jog down on the beach, and since I was passing by, I thought I'd come wake you up. Seems I achieved my goal."

He looked at me for a moment, then stretched and yawned. "I guess since you're taking on your wicked grandmother's tactics and waking me up too damned early, I should invite you in. You can make coffee while I shower."

I took his comment as one of affection toward my grandma rather than taking offense, and followed him into the house.

Drew left me in the kitchen, and I smiled when I realized the coffee was exactly where my grandma always kept it. However, the pot was significantly more complex than the old percolator she'd used when we were kids.

I struggled to figure out how to fill the damned thing, so it took almost the entire time Drew was showering to get the coffee on. When he came back down, he teased me about my ineptitude, and all I could do was chuckle.

"I probably should get back and shower myself," I said. "Don't want to be late for our date."

Drew's eyebrow crept up, but he didn't respond. That was good, at least. If he wasn't going to flat-out deny this was a date, I might have a chance of seeing the same look he gave me back in Salem. I might have a chance to feel what it was like to have those full lips on mine.

"No coffee first?" he asked.

"Well, maybe I have time for a cup, especially since it took so much effort to make it."

"Not everyone has an assistant to make their coffee, oh great attorney man. Now that you're in the country, you might have to figure some things out on your own."

It was my turn to cock an eyebrow. I was about to make a cutting retort, but just then, I noticed his playful smirk and a little spot of toothpaste on his bottom lip. I made to rub it off, and when it wouldn't budge, I stuck my thumb in his mouth to moisten it and back out to wipe the spot away.

When we made eye contact, his expression had taken on the sexy, hungry look I'd so desperately wanted to see again. When I leaned down to kiss him, however, he stepped back.

"Lance, there's no doubt we are attracted to each other, but if we indulge this, without thought, it's likely going to just be a quick fuck. Do you really want that? I mean, it's cool if you do, but we have a connection, because of how both of us feel about Gwen, and with the curse."

I sighed. "I don't know, but since you were at my home, I don't seem to be able to get you out of my head. Part of me wants to just have at it and see if that relieves some of this... I guess you could call it angst."

Drew laughed heartily. "Like, you're a teenager or something?"

I smiled. "Yeah, or something."

Drew stepped back into my space and pulled me down for a kiss. Although chaste, it sent electrical currents through me. When he pulled back, I could tell he was just as affected by it as I was.

He cleared his throat, and said, "Let's do this. You go back to the cottage and get ready, and I'll come pick you up, and then we'll see where it leads. At least that way, we'll have some time to really think this through."

"Like adults?" I asked, and he chuckled.

Then, his face became serious, and with squinted eyes that showed he was concentrating, he responded, "Well, like a couple people who have something to lose."

That cooled me off enough, so I nodded. "I'll see you in an hour then," I said, and turned to head out the door.

As I jogged back, I couldn't help but think how nice it would've been to wake up next to his warm body and cuddle him, then sit in my grandma's old kitchen and have coffee together. Not to mention having had delicious morning sex beforehand. Just thinking of the way his lips felt under my thumb as I rubbed it over his hot mouth sent shivers through my entire body. He was right, of course, about jumping into bed before we were ready, but damn, I couldn't imagine not having his body under mine at some point. It just seemed... meant to be.

Thirteen

Drew

"T HAT MAN UNSETTLES ME."

As soon as I'd said the words, I heard her chuckle. "Gwen, you're spying. That's creepy," I said, and the chuckle continued.

I closed my eyes, and focusing on my third eye, saw her sitting on the old stool she always sat on in the mornings.

You know if a man doesn't unsettle you in the early stages, he's not usually worth pursuing.

I just shook my head. *You're a ridiculous romantic, Gwen.*

She smiled. *You were right to hold off, though, get to know him first. Also...* she hesitated before continuing, *...you need to clear the air. I can feel the resentment every time you see him. You can't have a healthy relationship with someone, not even a strictly sexual one, when you harbor resentment. Besides, it's not entirely his fault that he wasn't here. I didn't want anyone but you around when I was sick. Forgive him and let it go.*

I sat across from her and sighed. *You knew this was coming.*

A sad smile crossed her face. *I saw it years ago when I first met you. At first I thought it was Kyle you'd end up with, but then I realized you are too... well, too much for poor Kyle. No, you need a man like my Lance.* She sighed heavily then, and looking down at her hands, continued, *I had hoped he'd come to his senses while I was still alive. I'd have enjoyed seeing the two of you working through your differences, and maybe playing matchmaker a bit, but it wasn't the right time. Neither of you were ready.*

You know I don't believe in destiny, Gwen, that's up to us.

You've preached that to me literally since the day we met, but there are people who are supposed to be in our lives. They complement us, fill us with purpose and meaning. Sometimes they cause us to grow and change. She shifted as she pondered what to say next. *You know that can be beautiful, like the friendship you and I had, but it can also be ugly and painful. Not unlike how your father influenced you. Regardless, you're a better man because of him, even though I know it hurts for you to see that.*

Gwen, you've been preaching that since I met you, and it doesn't hurt any longer. I feel the same as you, Lance is a part of me. Somehow, some way, but for certain, our paths were meant to cross.

We sat across from each other, and the contemplative silence between us reminded me of the many times we'd sat just like this and had similar conversations. When I'd first moved to Chemeketa, I was angry about my parents, blaming them for everything wrong in my life. However, Gwen had delicately and lovingly shown me that while I couldn't escape my past, I could choose a new path for myself. I was who I was because of my parents. No, they weren't good people. No, I didn't have to forgive them, but I could accept that I'd grown as a person, and a strong one at that, because of, and likely despite them.

I've already decided I'm willing to take him as my lover, I said to her, unsure how she would respond. Yes, she loved romance, but she also knew my history with men. Only a few had ever made it past my walls, and none had left the mark that others would call love.

She smiled, stood, and kissed me on the top of my head.

I'll leave it to you, but I will give you one warning. That's what scares his father's cantation the most. You are a danger to its very existence. Probably because of the years it's existed unchallenged, and because the boys believe in their father's curse, whether they admit it or not. That has made it very powerful. If you pursue this, you'll need to listen carefully to your heart, and not your fears about love. The cantation will challenge you every step of the way, searching for any cracks in the surface it can use to its advantage.

Gwen, are you going? I asked, and she smiled sadly.

Yes and no. I can't interfere with your relationship with my grandson, and even if I could, I wouldn't. I'm here if you need me. She hesitated for a moment. *Eventually, I'll grow weary of this life. Even now, I can feel the pull from across the veil, and eventually I'll have to answer that call, but for now, if you need me, I'm here.*

She turned toward her old bedroom as if she was going for a lie down, but glanced back before disappearing, and said, *I love you, Drew, like my own flesh and blood, so don't be offended when I say, don't let the walls keep you from feeling. Love is an emotion of the heart, not the mind. If you spend all your time analyzing everything, you prevent it from taking root. I honestly don't know whether Lance is the right seed for your heart or not, but give him a chance... if for no other reason, do that for me.*

She faded from sight then, a finality to it I hadn't felt before. A wave of grief struck me numb, almost like it had when she'd first passed away. I sort of hoped she was passing on, but at the same time, it hurt every part of me to lose her.

I pulled myself out of the trance, drank down the lukewarm coffee, and finished getting ready. It was time to put some of my resentments to bed once and for all. How Lance reacted to me would determine whether there was a path forward romantically or not. Regardless, Gwen was right. I needed to open myself up and dismantle the walls I'd built as a child to keep me safe. I was strong enough now to let myself be vulnerable. Whether that was vulnerable with Lance or someone else was yet to be seen. I was ready, though, either way.

Lance was just coming out of the little cottage when I pulled up to the door. His smile was bright despite the blustery morning. It almost got past the clouds in my mind, and that in and of itself was a miracle.

He'd just opened the passenger side door when he looked over at me, and a frown crossed his handsome face. "Have I upset you again?" he asked.

"No, get in, though. I need to have a serious conversation before we take this much further."

He nodded and climbed in.

"Lance, this isn't going to be easy to hear, but if there's a chance that we're going to be involved, be that as friends or more, I need to speak frankly with you about your grandmother." He nodded, encouraging me to continue, but still looking concerned. "You know Gwen was my best friend, I've told you that before. I watched her when you and your brothers avoided her, what it did to her. I saw the pain she felt when you'd find excuses not to visit her, and the only way she was ever able to see you was for her to go to you. I'll be honest, I harbor quite a lot of resentment over that."

I glanced over at him, and he seemed willing to hear me out, so I continued, "I can't blame you for not coming at the end. She didn't want you to see her after she got sick, and I'm fairly certain she'd put up barriers that kept you away by that point. But, before that, why did you stay away? Why did you leave her alone without the love of her family? And what took you so long to come collect the things she'd left for you? Before you answer, I know you don't owe me any explanations, but if you have any hope of being in any type of relationship with me, you'll have to communicate with me about it. I don't think I can forgive you without that."

A myriad of emotions crossed Lance's face as he found his voice. I recognized anger, then frustration and a flash of hurt, and when he reached resignation, I knew we were going to have a real conversation about this.

"This is difficult for me to talk about, Drew. I don't think I could've answered that before maybe even yesterday." He drew in a deep breath and let it out. "I'll admit, I have struggled trusting you, and the more I whittle that down, the more that looks like jealousy." He stared out the front window for a moment before seeming to make up his mind about something. "Why don't we go to the restaurant. I need coffee before I confess all my sins. Maybe some carb-filled crap food too, 'cause I'm gonna need some comfort food if I'm to put my insides out in the open."

I nodded and drove to the little restaurant in downtown Chemeketa. Amelia's had just opened for the day, which meant its namesake owner would be a little grumpy. Everyone in town knew the earlier you got there, the grumpier she was likely to be.

I let my heart guide me, and leaned over and kissed Lance on the cheek before getting out of the vehicle. "If it helps, I know this is hard. I had a shitty childhood myself, and there are places from my past I've never returned to, so I understand some of it. I just don't understand why you pushed someone who loved you so unconditionally out of your life."

Lance's eyes were clouded over, showing emotions that were deep and painful. I needed to remember that as we talked, this wasn't easy for him, and being pissed and unyielding would do nothing to help me understand. As we got out of the vehicle, I pulled in several breaths to steady myself and find the empathy inside me to understand where he was coming from, reminding myself the intention here was to let go of my resentment, not punish him for what I perceived as him being wrong.

As predicted, Amelia gave us the stink eye as we walked into the restaurant. Amelia was part of Gwen's coven, and I'd spent a lot of time with the woman. Knowing she was probably suffering from lower back pain, which tended to keep her up at night and led to much of her early morning moodiness, I told Lance to find a seat while I conjured up a silent warming remedy I'd used with her before.

I could tell she wanted to lash out, but when she saw me chanting, she smiled and turned, so I could access her sore muscles.

As usual, the moment I touched her lower back, her back adjusted and she moaned.

"Why don't you go to the chiropractor?" I asked.

"'Cause, I hate having someone crack on me, and anyway, we don't have one here."

Shaking my head at the stubborn woman, I said, "You should've called me when it started hurting. I could've at least done this for you."

"You know I don't like to be a bother. Besides, it's this blasted rain anyway, every year it takes me longer and longer to get used to the shift from summer to fall. If Chemeketa wasn't the only town with its own built-in witch's council, I'd consider moving to a drier climate."

"Well, that should help," I said, and she looked over my shoulder at Lance.

"Is that Gwen's grandson you've got with you?" she asked. The woman had a second sense about people.

"It is. Gwen's been pushing us together since she passed. He's staying over at the cottage for the next couple of weeks."

"Damn, is she still meddling? I thought she'd hang up that hat at least after death."

"I wouldn't hold my breath. That woman loves playing matchmaker, death doesn't have a chance keeping her from it."

"Why ain't he staying with you?" she asked.

Not surprised she knew the gossip, I sighed before responding, "'Cause, I'm not sure I'm ready to let Gwen's matchmaking stick or not. A man's got to have his agency, Amelia."

"Like you've ever said no to that woman. Besides, I may be a dyke, but even I can see he's a whole bunch of man candy!"

I burst out laughing, and Lance eyed us suspiciously.

"I could've died and gone across the veil and happily never heard those words come out of your mouth, Amelia." I leaned over and laid a kiss on her cheek, which always annoyed her. Amelia hated all forms of PDA.

"We're gonna work through some stuff, but he said he needs comfort food, and we're gonna need lots of coffee. Can you fix us up?"

"Sure, I think I remember what he ate when he was a boy."

"Hey, Lance, do you still like French toast stuffed with cream cheese?" she yelled across the restaurant.

He thought for a moment, and a smile crossed his face. "Yeah, and some of your chili-spiced bacon? Do you still make that?"

She chuckled. "Not in a long time, but I can whip some up for you."

"Thank you, Ms. Amelia," he said.

Amelia smiled at me, showing my conjuring had helped ease the pain, then got busy on our breakfasts while I went over to join Lance.

"I'm surprised she remembers me, it's been a long time since I've been in here. Hell, I was still just a kid then."

"Amelia's mind is like a steel trap, as are other elements of her personality. If she liked you, she'd remember."

"Doesn't she keep her coffee out here somewhere?" he asked. "I should've drunk what you offered me this morning instead of... well, instead of getting distracted. I'm beginning to get a headache."

I got up and went over to where Amelia kept her coffee pot and cups for the regulars to help themselves.

"Amelia decided after her daughter moved away that she wasn't going to hire anyone else, something about how kids these days couldn't do something or another. Anyway, she's basically trained all of us to wait on ourselves. She does the cooking and will bring it to you if she's not too busy. Otherwise, she just yells at you from the window to 'come get your own damned order'."

Lance chuckled. "Hey, it works for me. As long as I get some coffee in me. Didn't her wife help her in the restaurant?" he asked.

"She did, until she broke her hip a few years ago. Now it hurts her too much to stand. You know she's fifteen years older than Amelia, and Amelia isn't a spring chicken."

"You know I can hear y'all, right?" Amelia yelled from the kitchen.

"I know you're eavesdropping," I yelled back at her, earning me another chuckle from Lance.

"I wonder what else has changed since I was here. In my mind, Chemeketa is still like it was when I was growing up."

I shook my head. "Every place changes, it's just how the world works. Even though we're a small town steeped in tradition, not even we can escape it. The council meets frequently to discuss how to preserve our little town's ways, and keep ourselves relevant in modern times. We're a town of gifted people, and we certainly don't want to stand out, but if we don't change and adapt, we will."

Lance smiled. "It's exactly the same in every small town around here. Hell, I was in Florence just a couple weeks ago and sat through a town hall meeting where they were discussing that very issue."

"Yeah, historically, the coast wasn't that appealing, especially a town off in the middle of nowhere, but society has changed, and the coast has become far too interesting to weekenders. You know, people who just want a holiday pad or something. We have people constantly wanting to buy property here, wanting to change how we operate. I think every small tourist town struggles with that in one way or another, but Chemeketa struggles with it in rather unique ways too."

I didn't realize I was rambling, sharing things I'd never shared with an outsider, but Lance didn't feel like an outsider any longer. Something had changed. I wasn't sure if the change was in him or me. Regardless, until that very moment, I hadn't noticed it, but it felt like his energy was different now. Somehow, in my mind, he'd become one of us.

Amelia came out of the kitchen carrying two steaming plates, put the food in front of us, and winked at me as another customer came in.

I chanted a little rhyme.

"Close the door, and shut the curtains, this conversation's for us and no other person."

I felt the air shift around us, and Amelia looked over. Her smile quickly shifted from curious to naughty. I could only assume she figured we wanted to have a private conversation about things lovers would do. I ignored her and focused on Lance.

"Okay, this is private now. You can speak your mind, and no one will hear us."

Lance looked at me, brow furrowed. "What was that?"

"Just a little privacy spell. Amelia loves to hear the gossip, not that she repeats it, but I figured your experiences and thoughts were your own. I didn't want anyone listening in on what you had to say."

The curious look didn't leave his face, but he did sigh. "You asked why I didn't come to visit very often, why I let our grandmother die without coming to see her, and why I waited so long to deal with her stuff when it was over. I could use the excuse that it's because I moved so far away. Shortly after graduating law school, I moved to New York and started working as an attorney there. One thing led to another, and before I knew it, I was involved in politics and working with all sorts of politicians, including presidents, over the years."

He sat contemptibly, then sighed again. "But, the truth is, I was running away. I don't know how much my grandmother shared with you about our past, but I was actually close to my father for a long time. In fact, I idolized him growing up."

Lance stared down at his hands as he spoke, picking at his thumbnail cuticles. "My mom was cold even when we were young. I will never understand why she had kids, she certainly wasn't cut out for raising them. But my father was different, at least when we were young. He'd bring us to Chemeketa, and we'd play on the beach, hang out with our grandparents, explore the world."

Lance smiled briefly at what must've been a happy memory, before a frown took its place. "Back then..."He paused, making eye contact with me. "...he fully embraced his paganism, or was it witchcraft? I don't know, we never really named it, but we'd hang out with Grandma, and, before he died, Grandpa. They would cast spells and do strange things under the moon..."

Lance's face dropped as the conversation stalled, and I knew he was remembering things he'd purposely kept locked away for years. These were painful memories, and reliving them brought all those bottled feelings to the surface.

"Anyway, all that changed when I became a teenager. He finally let my mother and her parents talk him into going into politics, but he'd have to denounce his mother's ways. I can still remember the conversations and the horrible things my mother said about Chemeketa and our grandparents in particular. Dad ended up joining the Catholic church and set about becoming a *respectable* person. I'm not sure what happened over those next couple of years, but he changed. His spirit began to wither inside him. Where he'd once been a loving and gregarious man, similar to Grandma in most respects, he shifted and became more like my mother, more like her parents."

He shook his head as he spoke, and I didn't miss the slight tremble in his voice. "Dad stopped visiting Chemeketa and even stopped helping us with our homework or generally spending time with us. My great-grandfather, Grandma's father-in-law, was bisexual and being from here, that didn't matter really. Grandma told all three of us kids about it when we were still really young, about how he'd decided to marry a man instead of our grandpa's mom. The three of them lived together on the property you now own, if I remember the story correctly. So, when I started acknowledging that I preferred men over women, it didn't seem like a big deal. I never felt like I needed to come out."

"You thought the family history would cause him to support you," I murmured.

"Well, yes, and I was the oldest, so maybe it was simply something that I accepted, even if it wasn't spoken out loud, but Kyle... was different. He was enough younger than Crea and me that he hadn't been exposed to Chemeketa in the same ways we had. He was also more involved in the church, even attending Catholic boarding school for a while. Then one evening, in a fit of tears, he told us he thought he might be bisexual or gay. His school had actually forced all the students to attend a class about the evils of homosexuality, so he was afraid to tell our parents. I was such an arrogant ass, I just shrugged and said, 'You've got nothing to worry about. Our great-grandpa was bi and I'm gay, it's not a big deal in our family.' Kyle never really knew any of that and it shocked him."

"So, what happened?" I asked, now curious.

"More as a way to ease Kyle's concerns, I decided to come out to Mom and Dad. So, we all sat down for dinner that night and between 'pass the rolls' and 'what did you learn at school today?' I said, 'You all know I'm gay, right?'"

I smiled sadly because I could visualize that young, arrogant Lance just going about his life assuming the world was going to support him. And how crushing it must've been when he learned the opposite was true.

Lance's expression turned stony as he delved deeper into what I assumed was his worst memory. "Dad blew a gasket. We were shocked. How didn't he already know? Mom acted like she was about to faint, all a bunch of ridiculous drama but still overwhelming for us. I got up from the table to get away from them, but by the time I got to the living room, Dad had caught up to me. 'No son of mine is going to be with another man!' He screamed that at us, at me. I tried to lighten the mood, joking if he was planning to kill every guy I'd date, and he glared back as if it were a challenge."

Lance drew in a shaky breath as he fished something out of his pocket and began absently rolling it with his fingers. Gwen's ring. I was glad to see he'd taken my advice to carry it with him. "Things escalated quickly after that. Crea ended up telling him he was gay, and then poor Kyle came out too, and well, you can guess how well that went over. I was about to walk away again when my dad's face *changed*. The words to his chant are etched in my brain, but I swore I'd never repeat them, never say them out loud. I think deep down I hoped that by not acknowledging them, not believing in them, it'd mean they weren't real."

I wanted to reach out and take his hand, just as a support, but instinctively I knew he needed to get this out first before I could touch him.

"I'd been my grandmother's shadow most of my child-hood, so I knew chants and spells. They came into my head with little to no effort, and after our father cursed us, I tossed one back at him. He'd taken love away from us, and I returned the favor. He would never know the love of his children ever again, and it worked, Drew. It *worked*. The feelings I'd had for my father, all the love I'd felt up until that point, were gone in an instant, and I'd done that... I'd cursed us as much as he had."

A few tears escaped his eyes and rolled down his face. He wiped at them, before continuing, "Dad ended up hitting me, and I fell and split my head open on a coffee table in our living room. He said then because blood was spilled, the curses were cast. That's the last time I saw him. I was rushed to the hospital, and our grandmother came to pick us up. We stayed with her after that, and when I left for college, I never looked back. Somehow, Grandma and Chemeketa had collapsed with the hor-rors of that day. I'm not sure about my brothers. I assume it's the same for them, since they rarely visited either. We've never spoken about any of it... that day, the curses, or the loss of our parents."

I pushed our plates aside, then reached over and final-ly took his hand. "I understand a little more now, but you know Gwen adored you, and she talked about the three of you incessantly. In her mind, you never stopped being part of her family, part of her life. Just seeing that hurt me for her. And I hated you for it."

Lance nodded, then locked eyes with me. "Last night was the first night since then that I accepted that I allowed my father to push me away from all the people and places I loved. I did love this place, and Grandma was... she *is* my family. I thought I was in control by keeping everyone at arm's length, but I see now that was part of his hatred. I'd given all my power... all my ability to love away, just because he stole it from me."

The two of us sat across from each other for a long time, neither of us talking or eating our food, but still holding hands.

I finally broke the silence. "Lance, my father beat me for as long as I can remember growing up. He hated me. He'd tell me I was taking my mother from him. The Department of Children's Services would get involved occasionally, but they'd always send me back. When I was a teenager, I ran away, and he ended up killing my mother and himself. I know what it's like to have someone control you through fear. I'm sorry you didn't let Gwen back into your life before she passed. She's such an amazing human being and I feel lucky to have had her in mine."

I stared out over the restaurant, remembering the first day I met her. "I was a snot-nosed kid who was learning paganism to basically get even with my dad, who'd clutched his religion to him and wielded it like a weapon. When I met Gwen, the world began to right itself. She became my light and has been ever since. If it wasn't for her, I'd still probably be that broken young man she found at the pagan camp, scrubbing toilets and mowing fields to avoid starving to death. She helped me see that I could accept the good people gave me and cast off the bad." He squeezed my hand in support, as I continued, "It sounds like your father was a good man before and that you loved him." I smiled at the fact that what I was going to say next was so quintessentially Gwen. "You can embrace that part of him, pull it into your heart and nurture it, and you can just as powerfully cast off the hatred. Curses are only powerful when we believe in them. They're conquered through our abilities to see past the pain into the light." Another tear had slipped down Lance's face, and this time I reached across with my other hand and wiped it away. "Let the light in now. No more darkness, okay?"

"You sound like her," he said, which caused me to choke up for a moment.

"That's a high compliment. She's clearly a part of both of us, huh?" I asked.

Lance let go of my hand as he leaned back in his chair, and the serious air around us began to soften. He took a bite of his food and frowned. "French toast isn't very good cold."

I moved my hand in a counterclockwise direction reversing the silence spell, then waved my hands over our food.

Lance's eyes grew wide, and he sampled the French toast again. "It's hot! How do you do that?"

I shrugged, but couldn't hold back a smirk. I didn't mind impressing him, even if it was with a basic skill. "Simple energy movement. Causing something to heat up is the easiest spell of all." I glanced over my shoulder, and seeing that Amelia was within earshot, said, "Keeping busybodies out of your business, now that's a difficult spell."

Amelia turned around and stuck her tongue out at me, causing both Lance and I to laugh out loud.

Fourteen

Lance

THE AIR CLEARED QUICKLY after we'd finished *Confessions with Drew*, as I'd dubbed this morning's conversation over breakfast. Surprisingly, it was easy to tell Drew what had happened with my dad, even if it *was* the first time I'd ever told anyone other than Grandma. Over the years, when the few people close to me had asked about my parents, I simply told them they struggled with my being gay. No one ever asked any further questions, and until now, that was how I liked it.

That being said, after sharing everything with Drew, it was like a light had been shone into a dark place, into my soul. The magic of that was something I could easily believe in. I felt freer than I could remember feeling, and all because I had enough strength, finally, to confess what had really happened to me that day.

After breakfast, he drove me back to his place. We walked down to the beach and along the area where an ancient volcanic lava flow once poured into the sea. There were few remnants of the flow except some rocks worn down by the waves.

The side of the mountain was exposed, and the black rock sometimes glistened in the sun. When we were little, Crea and I pretended it sparkled because diamonds that only we could see were stuck in the mountain.

As we walked, I became more nostalgic. I kicked my shoes off and began running in the fishy-smelling surf, taunting Drew, who quickly did the same. We chased each other, laughing until my feet were so cold I could barely feel them.

"It's been a long time since I did that," I admitted, and lay back on the dry sand that had been warmed by the late morning sunshine.

Drew plopped down beside me and just stared up at the sky, not really responding to my comment. We were lying close on the sand, the heat radiating off him warming my cold body. I leaned up on my elbow, looking down at him, and when he rolled toward me, I leaned over and kissed him.

When I pulled back, Drew's eyes were closed, but a smile slowly crept across his face. "That was nice, but didn't really last long enough," he said.

He opened his eyes then and pulled me down into a kiss, this time deepening it, forcing his tongue into my mouth, and all of a sudden, my body didn't feel so cold anymore.

FIFTEEN

DREW

I REACHED DOWN AND scooped up a handful of sand, drawing in the essence of the millions of years of erosion that it'd taken to form. *"Praeteritum ad praesens,"* I whispered, Latin for *bring the past to the present*, then threw the sand toward the four corners of the earth. I hardly ever used Latin, even though I'd had to learn it as a child, but for a spell that basically hid you in the folds of time, it seemed... appropriate.

I stripped my shirt off and challenged Lance to do the same. "Here?" he asked as his eyes darted around the deserted beach. I was surprised he didn't comment about the chant.

"No one's around, and I've... protected our privacy," I said.

Lance hesitated, then shrugged before stripping off his shirt and scooting back into my space.

"Oh gods, your body feels nice," I said when his warm skin touched my own.

Lance hummed in agreement as he unbuckled my pants.

Our mouths met as he stripped my pants off, leaving me naked against the sand. I seldom wore underwear these days, hating to do any more laundry than absolutely necessary.

"You too!" I demanded, and Lance complied, surprising me that he trusted we were safe. Maybe our talk this morning had really gotten through to him.

The moment he was naked, he bent down and took me in his mouth.

"Oh fuck!" I moaned as his warm mouth expertly sucked me deep into his throat. "Fuck yeah, Lance..."

I was so close, I had to gently push him off. He smirked and turned his body, so he was kneeling above my head. At my nod, he eased his cock in my mouth, then bent over sixty-nine style and began blowing me again.

My gods, it'd been so long since I had another man's cock in my mouth, and Lance's cock was perfect—thick and long. When he rocked his hips and hit the back of my throat, I saw stars. Gods, I so loved to have my mouth fucked.

"Mmm," I moaned around him.

The need to come overtook me, and I tried to pull away, but Lance held onto me, sucking harder and fucking my mouth with the same intensity.

"Aaah," I said around his cock as I unloaded in his mouth. Seconds later, he returned the favor, and I eagerly swallowed his load. Even if I wasn't attuned to the earth and the air around me, I would've felt the magic of the moment.

Lance sat up and repositioned his sand-covered body next to mine, then pulled me close.

With one arm wrapped around Lance, I waved my other hand, gathering the warmth from the sun around us. Heat seeped into the sand where we lay, warming us up as if we were lying on a Southern California beach and not an Oregon beach in the fall.

Within seconds, Lance was snoring lightly beside me.

I watched him as he slept. No man had ever intrigued me as much as he did. His mouth was slightly parted, and he breathed heavily. I couldn't resist, so I leaned over and kissed him.

I could feel a gentle smile spread across his face before he returned the kiss. "I fell asleep," he said as I trailed light pecks down his neck.

"Good sex will do that for you."

"I need more good sex then," he said, pulling me into his chest. My arms automatically wrapped around him in an embrace, and we sat like that for a moment, just enjoying the feel of each other.

"Wanna do it again?" he asked as I let him go, and I laughed.

"Maybe later. I have to meet the town council in an hour, and I should get showered and dressed."

"Mmm, I could help with the shower."

I couldn't help the smile that crossed my face. "That's a great idea, then I want you to come to the meeting with me. I'd like you to meet the townsfolk."

He cocked an eyebrow at me. "Um, why?"

"Well, because it's been a long time since you were in town, and it'd be good for you to meet some of the folks who make Chemeketa what it is. I'd also like to show you off."

He looked momentarily surprised at my declaration before his lips quirked into a satisfied smirk, and he shrugged. "Show me off, huh? Why not? It isn't like I haven't had to sit through a million of these types of meetings anyway."

I kissed him again and got up, pulling him with me as we walked naked back to the house, dragging the invisibility spell with us. We were still covered with sand and went directly into the outdoor shower. Of course, I knew this wasn't going to be just a shower.

Once the water warmed up, he stepped in behind me and began lathering my body.

If the sex on the beach had been good, this was everything I wanted and more. "I've been tested, and I'm negative, you?" he asked.

"No sex in years, tested and negative as well."

His soapy hands continued sliding across my wet skin as he moved around to my front to lather my chest. "Can we?" he asked, looking into my eyes. I knew he wanted to know if we could be intimate without condoms.

When I nodded, he smiled, and reached around me to lather my backside.

He quickly moved behind me again and I moaned, loving the way his big fingers felt as they slipped in and out of my ass. I was so far removed from dating or hookups that I felt uncomfortable going all the way.

I felt Lance's cock brush against my ass, then he slowly moved in and out of my crack.

"Tease," I said, and hungry for more, pushed back until his cockhead slipped inside me.

Lance's hands snuck around my body, and he whispered into my ear, "You're so... so..."

I stopped his search for words by pressing into him, taking his cock as deep inside me as I could without him thrusting.

"Fuck!" he said, and began to pump into me.

"Yes, fuck me, Lance," I said, and he happily complied.

I knew if I hadn't been in a shower, I'd have been covered with sweat. The sex was overwhelming, matched only by the power pulsating between us. I'd never experienced anything like it, as if someone had flipped on a switch that was sending out arcs of electricity.

"I'm coming, Drew," he said, and remembering how amazing it'd been to swallow him while we'd sucked each other off on the beach, when Lance pulled out, I knelt down and let him come on my face.

His body pulsated under the water as the white ropes of cum briefly coated my face before the shower washed them away.

He pulled me up, then knelt down himself before taking my cock into his mouth. He sucked until I surrendered to my orgasm and once again emptied myself into his mouth.

As we approached the old Grange House, I could feel Lance tensing up. I pulled him aside before going in and asked what was going on.

"I'm just nervous for some reason. Grandma was a member of the council for many years. She'd sometimes bring us with her to help with chores around the Grange House. I remember the members were friendly, but that's part of why I struggle with it. My world today is so different from what it used to be. I'm almost afraid my good memories will be challenged by coming back here."

"Memories are moments in time and yours to keep. You shouldn't let whatever happens today cloud the innocence of your childhood. Things will be different, guaranteed, because you're different." I leaned over and kissed him, and said, "Come on, many of the folks you remember will still be here."

"Why are you needed tonight?" he asked.

"They're reconfiguring the Air Guild. Unfortunately, we've lost a few people recently, and our little Guild is suffering because of it."

"Air Guild?" His face registered confusion.

"Yeah, remember, we were founded by a group of Victorian witches. Instead of voting based on where we live in town, we're divided up by the different elements. Air, Water, Fire, and Earth. Our mayor is also on the council, so that makes five representatives."

"Okay, but... isn't that strange?" he asked.

"Well, maybe, but it's worked for over a century. I'm thinking it'll keep working."

As we walked in, Katan Manning met us.

"Well, Lance Franklyn, it's a pleasure to see you again after all these years."

Lance stared at Katan for several moments before recognition dawned and he nodded. "I remember you. Don't you own the old hardware store?"

Katan chuckled. "I used to own it. My son took it over a few years back. I took your grandma's place as mayor when she retired from the position, and that's all I have the energy for these days."

Lance shook hands with the mayor, and the concern that had been a cloud over him since I talked him into coming seemed to shift away.

"Oh, we're so happy to have your brother back in town, Lance, and now to have you back."

Lance chuckled. "Well, I'm only here visiting."

That caused the old man's expression to change, like a light had gone out. I almost laughed out loud, because I could all but read his thoughts. The older generation was looking for their replacements, maybe a little late considering most of them were well into their seventies, and no doubt ol' Katan thought he'd just found his. "Well, we're very thankful to have you back, even for a short time."

Sixteen

Lance

T HE MEETING WAS CALLED to order, and the discussion went immediately to Drew.

"So, what has the Air Guild decided regarding the council seat?" Donna Rummel asked. I remembered Donna from my childhood, and even then, she'd had the strongest personality in any room. Well, next to my grandma anyway. Donna's name plate noted her position as the representative from the Earth Guild.

"As you know, we don't work as fast as the rest of you," Drew said. "Our Guild needs time to discuss and consider all the aspects before we can elect our representative. I've been asked by the Guild to sit temporarily on the council until a suitable replacement has been found."

"Why don't you take the position full-time?" Donna asked.

Drew shrugged. "I've always traveled too much to be reliable. My band and I have just agreed to accept gigs overseas again. For now, though, I'll be around enough to help."

That mollified the group. Even though I had little to no connection to these people, even I believed Drew would probably never leave the position now that he'd taken it on. If his relationship with my grandmother had shown me anything, it was that he was dependable.

The rest of the council meeting was about issues that seemed to plague every small town in the state. I smiled at a few of them, like tourism, and keeping the town clean, that I'd heard multiple times in meetings such as this.

Before the meeting was concluded, the mayor paused for a moment.

"As you all know, I'll be turning eighty this summer. My wife has been harassing me to resign for over a decade, but I've resisted, at least until now. As is our custom, the mayor should have a year with an apprentice before handing over the reins. I was Gwen's apprentice before I took on the role," he said, then looked over at me.

I knew the next statement was being made for my benefit and I had to stifle my chuckle. "Our small town is unique, and as such, the leader requires special skills to manage it and keep it safe. In recent years, there have been other changes as well. Challenges that require a legal mind to negotiate with the state and federal powers."

Katan glanced at me again and smothered his own smile. "I'd ask that the council begin the process of identifying my replacement."

Then he sat down, and as I looked around the room, I could see several startled faces. So, it wasn't planned. My grandmother was so much like this guy. When she'd decided something should be a certain way, she'd basically made it happen. I looked to the ceiling, and conjuring her in my head, I said, *This is your training coming out, Grandma. I can feel it.* Katan continued to glance at me as the meeting wound down, and I knew I needed to do something to quell his thoughts.

"If that's the conclusion of our meeting—" Donna finally said, "—then I need to get home. I've got the Earth Guild coming over tonight to prep for the Harvest Moon Festival."

The mayor waved his hand and cheerfully closed the meeting.

After Drew introduced me to a few more people, he was immediately pulled into a conversation with Abigale Scott and her father, Owen, who represented the Water Guild, as well as Rose Shepherd, leader of the Fire Guild.

I began helping put the chairs away, a chore that was more muscle memory than something someone asked me to do.

Katan came up and cleared his throat, and I turned to see the older man standing nervously behind me.

"I hope I didn't make you too uncomfortable," he said.

I regarded him a moment, before I finally said, "You think I'm going to fill the position you mentioned?"

"I know it sounds odd, considering all your experiences, but there are a lot of issues that need to be addressed that you can't learn outside this community," he explained.

I chuckled. "Mr. Manning, I'm not moving to Chemeketa. I'm only visiting. I'm sorry if I gave you the wrong impression."

He nodded as though he understood before a smile spread across his face. "Son, I've been around a long time, and since my elemental sign is air, not different from yours, I've seen many people blow into town. I know which ones stay and which ones blow away again. You may not know it yet, but you are a stayer."

I wanted to argue that I had a job, but in fact, that wouldn't be the case soon enough since I wasn't running for reelection.

"I'm only scheduled to be here for a couple weeks of vacation before I'm back at work in Salem. I can't commit to anything at this point. I'm sorry," I said.

"I don't make things happen, my boy. I just see them. When the time is right for you, let me know, and I'll begin the transition process."

"Isn't the mayor of Chemeketa elected?" I asked before he was able to walk away.

"Of course, we're a democracy just like all towns in the US, but this town has always had its own trajectory. The townspeople tend to vote according to the best interests of the entirety. They'll want someone who knows the processes, and who's been recommended by the current mayor."

He walked away then, but not before he gave me a final wink.

Drew came over and patted my back. "Sorry, I see you've been, um, chosen."

I just shook my head. "Did you do that on purpose?"

Drew laughed and put his hands up. "No, not at all, but I'll be honest, I don't mind the pressure being taken off of me and put on you for a moment. I'm in no way cut out to be a politician, even in Chemeketa. I'm too opinionated and have no diplomacy skills. I'm more like a fire sign in that way than air."

I sighed and shook my head. "Oh, well, nothing to do about it. I'll be gone in a couple weeks anyway. Although, if my grandmother is still around, I'm almost sure she's enjoying this."

"No doubt," Drew said, and still smiling, escorted me out of the building.

Seventeen

Drew

I REALIZED TOO LATE I'd drawn Lance into a difficult situation. I really had just wanted him to be around the townspeople again, especially since we'd taken things to the next level. I loved this town, and these people were like family, so naturally I wanted him to be with me when I went to do my duties. I also knew he was a politician of sorts, so it just made sense to drag him to the council meeting.

The moment Katan saw him, though, I felt the energy shift. Energies were funny. They didn't operate on our timelines. Most of the time, things brewed under the surface long before we ever knew it was happening.

Katan had abdicated at that moment, and as far as Chemeketa was concerned, the shift of power from him to Lance had begun. Lance, of course, had his agency and could refuse it, but I knew, even without divination skills, that he wouldn't. Everyone in that room knew it too, and it was just a matter of time now before the entire town did.

What did that mean for me? For us? I wasn't sure. In a way, it was good. We needed strong leadership, and someone like Lance would be good for the community. Not just because of his political ties but because his mind, not unlike his grandmother's, was made for this type of position. Not to mention, Gwen had served as Chemeketa's mayor for many years.

No one was vying to replace Katan, though. Power in our community was garnered, not in positions, but in skill and practice, and with all the powerful witches in our midst, someone power-hungry would be sniffed out in a moment, and cast aside before they'd even get the chance to express an interest. The question for the people of our community would always be more about who was *right* for the position.

After the meeting, I decided I should begin showing Lance how to use some of his powers in order to help keep himself safe. He could do basic air spells without chanting. Just burning herbs and offering prayers were powerful enough for a lay practitioner. If he showed an interest in anything beyond that, well, we could work on that too. I didn't want to push him more than was necessary. It really could just be up to him.

After we ate dinner, I told him I wanted to show him some basics as a means of protecting himself, to which he didn't really complain.

"These are the herbs and even some spices I use for my spellcasting, and before you get all bent out of shape, I'm not asking you to do anything besides ask a simple prayer."

He chuckled, then kissed me. "I'm willing to let you show me."

"Good, come with me," I said, and brought him over to my side of the kitchen island. "Okay, tell me what concerns you most right now regarding your father's cantation."

He took a deep breath and thought for a moment. "Well, to be honest, I feel violated. It's like he's got access to me in a way he shouldn't."

I nodded as I considered his words. "So, there are many types of spells. There's the kind where you manipulate the elements like I did to warm up your food, which are basic physics. Excited neutrons make things warm. Then, there's the more complicated spells, like I cast when I wanted privacy for us at the restaurant and on the beach. Manipulating time isn't that difficult, it just involves causing waves to move a little differently than normal," I said, and got a naughty smile from him. "You can learn those too, but they're more advanced ,and require a lot of practice and concentration. I have to be in a constant state of awareness to cast those spells, especially manipulating time. Pushing things too far or doing too much could have serious consequences..." I'd seen others learn that lesson the hard way. Lance nodded, prompting me to continue, "Another type is chanting spells, which are fairly common in Wicca. They often rhyme, and that's on purpose, because for some reason, rhyming is basal in our human minds. We use rhymes to teach children to speak and write, and it's also a powerful way to focus your intentions..."

I paused to check that he was still following, and then remembered the night he almost died. "The night I came into your house, the darkness was everywhere, and I was afraid. I couldn't use higher magic, because... well, the fear caused me to lose my grasp on my consciousness. Really, Lance, that's not uncommon, we're still human, and humans are susceptible to their emotions, so we need something basic to fall back on. That's where chanting comes in. It's a way for us to force ourselves out of our primitive minds and back into a state of spiritual consciousness."

Seeing he was confused, I sighed. I knew I was asking a lot for him to understand all this, but at least he was now receptive to hearing it. "I chanted that your father's dark energy be cast away, and drew upon your grandmother's energy to help me. The chanting allowed me to stay focused on the intention, on the task at hand. It gave me something to hold onto. Does that make sense?"

Lance stared at me a moment, his brow furrowed, then nodded. "I mean, you know I don't want to believe in this stuff, but I guess I always have. Yes, it makes sense, and I've used that kind of magic myself. In fact, it's what I used when I cast my father's curse back onto him."

I leaned over and into his side. "I'm sorry, Lance. I know that has to make this hard."

I turned to face him then, and when he made eye contact, I said, "But... you must be able to protect yourself, and as the de facto leader of the Air Guild, and you being an air sign, it's my job to tutor you, at least until someone else takes up the job."

He grinned at me, which I took to mean he liked the idea of us spending more time together. "A prayer is basically an intention, spoken or thought. Every religion seems to use similar tactics. For example, incense is often burned when you ask a prayer. Paganism has something quite similar. Instead of using premade incense, however, we tend to use our own herbs."

I began to move the herbal containers around for a little show-and-tell. "Herbs and spices tend to be used more by earth practitioners, but others use them too. For air, once an item burns, its elements are shifted into smoke, or if you are using water, it's turned to steam. It shifts from the physical into a form that becomes part of the air around us." I looked into his face, saw the glazed eyes, and sighed. "I know I'm getting technical, but trust me, it's basically just elementary school science. Bear with me."

Lance chuckled. "Okay, tell me what to do with all this," he said, pointing at all the herbs.

"Yeah, okay. Think about your father. Think about all the frustration and feeling of being violated. Now pick out five or six herbs that feel right to create a protection around you."

I could tell Lance wanted to argue, but after a second, he began smelling the herbs and spices, and putting aside the different containers I assumed he thought would work.

"Perfect," I said when he stopped and looked at me. "The funny thing is, these are herbs and a spice known for their protective qualities."

I picked up the cinnamon, and said, "Any tree is known as a sentinel. Their roots either run deep or link together with other roots along the surface, so the bark of a tree, like cinnamon, will always be a good choice for a protection spell. I'll spare you going through the others, because, well, you get the point. But, at some point, it would do you good to study up on the herbs, to get the concepts of what the earth elementals use them for. You will, of course, always use your intuition, but learning about them is like checking your work."

Lance smiled at me, like an adult would when they were placating a child. I ignored it and began to combine the different herbs and spices he'd collected into the wooden mortar I kept in the kitchen for that purpose.

"Now, follow me outside," I said, as we made our way out to the garden. "Protection also comes from belief, and picking things that represent protection can be just as important as using herbs and spices that have spiritual elements to them. For example..." "I took my knife out of my pocket and sliced off a small section of the rose bush that grew next to the back door. "...roses have thorns, which protect the bush from predators. So, using a small section of thorns helps *represent* what you're striving for–protection."

I did the same thing with various other plants until I could tell I'd gotten my point across.

"Now, you go inside and grab us both a beer, or wine if you prefer, while I get a fire started."

He nodded and disappeared into the house. I didn't have the desire to waste time getting a fire going the traditional way, so I went to the fire pit, added some wood, and cast a spell instead. With the fire crackling, I looked back toward the house and saw Lance staring at me, his mouth a perfect "o" and a beer in each hand.

I shrugged. "Fire is easy for an air sign. Air feeds fire, so it usually comes to me without having to be too focused. Anyway, have a seat, we'll let the wood catch and make some coals before we begin the ritual."

We each sat in the comfortable Adirondack chairs next to the fire pit. "So, how did you get out of work for two weeks? I heard you tell Katan you planned to be here that long."

"Not much gets past you, does it?" he asked with a chuckle.

"I mean, I don't intentionally pay attention to other people's business, but after having mind-blowing sex twice in one day, a person is entitled to listen for how long more sex might be available."

Lance laughed. "I'm not running for reelection again. I'm tired of the rat race. So, knowing I'll have to begin the process of preparing my office for a transition soon, I knew I had this one chance to take time off before I became buried in work."

"Makes sense. So, you can just be away from your office for two weeks?" I asked.

"Yes, but I'll have to work some too. There are things that'll have to be dealt with whether I'm there in person or not. But I won't have to go to any boring meetings, and I can work from here."

I reached over and took his hand. "I'm glad. I'd like to show you some things around here you might've missed, and we do have one of our big festivals coming up as well. It's a good time to be in Chemeketa."

The coals had begun to glow, so I sat up and spread them out to create space for the items we'd gathered and visibly see them as they burned.

"Okay," I said and handed the mortar to Lance. "Think about what prayer you want to make. It doesn't *have* to rhyme. It doesn't have to even be much of anything other than, *keep me safe, please*, but you need to hold that thought or intention in your mind."

I waited while he thought. "Got it?" I asked, and he nodded. "Now, you can either speak it aloud or in your head as you pour the contents of the mortar onto the coals. It's important to watch the items burn while you quietly hold the intention in your mind."

He leaned up without my asking, poured the contents onto the fire, and mumbled something I wasn't able to hear.

Power washed over me, causing my head to spin. I was surprised, not that the spell was any less powerful than the others, but because Lance was so new, I didn't figure he'd pull such power from around him.

I looked over and saw he had his eyes closed and was mumbling under his breath.

Moments later, the contents that'd begun to burn sent up larger, more intense flames. As the heat increased, a small tornado began to swirl in the fire.

I looked over at Lance, who now had his eyes open, but his lips were still moving. The fire whirl began to reach higher, and when I was afraid it was about to set a nearby tree ablaze, I waved my hand to collapse it, but not before it sent sparks scurrying toward the sky.

"Um, what was that?" I asked. He returned my gaze, but his eyes were unfocused. "Lance," I said, clapping my hands. "Come back!"

He jerked and shook his head. "What... what happened?"

"You were spellcasting, and it was getting out of control. When's the last time you cast a spell?" I asked, both shocked and excited.

"Um, when I cursed my father."

"Well, you're powerful, Lance. More than someone should be after not working with energy for so long."

He shook his head. "It felt like someone else took over."

"Did someone? Did you feel your dad, or another entity take over?" I asked, feeling concerned.

He shook his head again. "No, it's just I've never felt that way, not even when I was young. Grandma would show me stuff, but it never felt like that."

I fell back into the chair and smiled. "Well, if that small prayer cast was any indication, showing you how to use your skill is going to be fun." I leaned up and took his hand in mine. "But, only if you want to, Lance. I'm not ever going to push you to do something you aren't ready for. You can tell me no at any time."

Shock still registered on his face, but I could also see glimpses of joy, the kind of joy one only got when the elements danced because of your intentions. I sort of knew it would be far from the last time he'd want to try something, but the choice was his, and as far as I was concerned, always would be. That didn't mean I didn't hope he wanted more, because I knew deep inside, the more the man got a grip on his power, the more fun we'd have as we explored one another.

EIGHTEEN

LANCE

THE MOMENT I POURED the herbs and spices we'd collected over the coals and prayed that my father's
hate be kept at bay, a strange warm sensation came over
me. I continued repeating the prayer over and over, and
the warmth began to transform into exhilaration.

It was like I told Drew. I felt like a passenger inside
a car. I was moving, but it was as if someone else was
driving.

Luckily, Drew pulled me back, because I got a bit
carried away, and before I realized it, the fire had gotten
big, too big. When Drew's energy swept into mine to
shut it down, I felt him. *Really* felt him.

It was almost as if I was inside his mind, even for just a
split second, but long enough to know the goodness that
permeated his consciousness. Any lingering concerns I
might've had about Drew were now gone. He was pure
light... or more accurately, he was a breath of fresh air.

The question was if it would it be enough to trust him.
Bitter memories of trusting my cheating ex-husband,
Tom, flashed powerfully into my mind. It was hard to
push them back, but now I could feel my father's curse

laced with the images. The years I'd spent ignoring my doubt, missing the signs of Tom's deceit... it was becoming clear the curse had been fueling my bad taste in men all along.

Then, there was Drew, a good man who'd wholeheartedly loved my grandma, and, in some ways, was just as eccentric. Was I ready to place my trust, my heart, in another man? Not that he'd asked me to throw caution to the wind and marry him, we were just getting to know each other. No need to put too much on this yet, right?

The elemental aspects my grandmother used to teach me were coming back. Even the things Drew had talked about and shown me were beginning to make more sense. When we connected, I could feel the air element inside him and for the first time, I could feel it inside myself as well.

How did that make me feel? I wasn't sure... not yet. But I did know for sure I wanted more of it. I was no longer afraid, though I couldn't say why exactly my fear had subsided. I just hoped this powerful feeling didn't end up being the end of me.

My father's powers had cursed me and my brothers to lives of loneliness. I guessed as things were clearing up in my head, I could see it. My father's and grandmother's skills weren't to blame so much as bad choices... dark choices on his part. Just like anything, if used for an evil purpose, you got an evil outcome. What had happened tonight, with the prayer and the fire, that wasn't evil, that was... well, it was just... right.

"Harvest Moon Festival?" I asked again.

Drew nodded and laughed. "Lance, you can't tell me your grandmother didn't bring you to the festival. It's one of the most important days of the year here in Chemeketa. Besides, some Christian faiths celebrate it too."

"Yeah, but not my parents, and if I came to the festival, I was too young to remember. So, it's this weekend?"

"Yep, in less than a week. So, you should come help me and the Air Guild get ready."

I must've looked hesitant because Drew chuckled. "It won't be too difficult, we'll all work as a team and just use you as a beast of burden."

"Well, I guess that's okay, but does that mean you're gonna ride me later?"

I winked and sipped my beer as Drew's face drew into a smile as he thought about it.

"Well," he said, and pulled me up out of my chair. "For now, I have duties, which means you have duties, so come on."

We went to the Grange House, where the small group of elderly townsfolk representing the Air Guild were sitting in folding chairs outside the front door.

Drew introduced me to each of them, and although I didn't recognize anyone, I did feel a connection. I just assumed that was because I was an air energy as well.

When the crew sent us off on an errand that put us far enough away from them they wouldn't hear, I whispered, "Are all the Air Guild people that old?"

Drew looked serious as he nodded. "Yeah, air signs don't usually stay in one place long. We are and always have been more nomadic than the other signs, except for water, of course. They are who we have left here in Chemeketa."

"I can see why they asked you to take over," I said, and he did chuckle then.

"So, they will want the kites to be placed in that area," he said, changing the subject.

"Kites? Isn't this the wrong time of the year?" I asked.

Drew got a mischievous look on his face, flipped his hand, and a breeze swept past me, lifting my hair.

"Not a problem, trust me."

"I guess that's one of the benefits, huh?"

"One of the many," he said, and began prepping the area. "We'll put the kites out that morning, because, for real, it will rain between now and then. We'll all get together the morning of the festival and work on creating a break in the weather if we do end up having a rainy day."

"Um, you mean change the weather?" I asked, shocked and a little bit alarmed.

Drew shrugged. "It's not hard. Clouds bring rain and cold. You create a blockage, and the rain just goes around it."

"I know a lot of politicians who'd like to possess that kind of power."

"And, that's not gonna happen. We've taken an oath to avoid giving power to the... power-hungry."

"I haven't."

"No," Drew said, and looked sad for a moment. "Not all practitioners make that oath, but if you were to come back to Chemeketa or join a coven, they'd require it."

"I'm happy to take an oath not to give politicians anything magical. Trust me, I know firsthand what many if not most would do with it."

Drew came over and kissed me, a huge smile on his face. "That's reassuring, but, for now, there's no concern for oaths or joining things. All we need to focus on is getting this area set up for Saturday."

Nineteen

Drew

My first thought when Lance mentioned politicians wanting to know how to control the weather was to freak out. I might've stopped all the training then and there had it been anyone but him. Luckily, he quickly confirmed politicians weren't usually reliable enough to wield that sort of power. I just had to trust that Gwen wouldn't have led him into my path had she not believed he was someone with integrity.

People who could do what we did should never be put in positions where greed could overtake their common sense.

I managed to shake off my concerns and enjoy the rest of the morning. Lance and I had spent a week just enjoying each other's company. I'd shown him how to utilize the chanting spells as well as the prayer spells and had told him, eventually, if he kept practicing, the ability to wave his hand to cast a spell would come in time.

One night, as we sat in the living room staring into the fireplace, I felt Gwen's presence, and nudged Lance. "Your grandmother is here, wanna see her?" I asked.

Lance's eyes grew large. "Um, yeah? Can you do that?" he asked.

"Close your eyes," I told him, and he immediately complied. I smiled, knowing how far we'd come that he trusted me enough just to go with it.

"Envision a third eye in the middle of your forehead, nod when you can see and feel it."

He nodded almost immediately. "Now, look through that eye," I said.

He tensed and sucked in a breath, and I knew he saw her. I closed my eyes and joined him in the trance.

When I glanced over at Lance, tears were slipping down his face. *Hello, Grandson*, Gwen said, the same tears of happiness flowing from her.

I sat quietly watching the two reunite. Lance kept apologizing for not being here, and Gwen kept telling him it was okay. Finally, she drew him into her arms. Emotions were more palpable in this type of trancelike state, and I could feel the healing that was happening between them.

When I began to leave, Gwen reached over and put her hand over mine. She shook her head, telling me to stay.

When they finally pulled apart, Gwen sat on the coffee table that was in front of us. *I need to warn you that your father is near. I feel the darkness gathering around Chemketa, but... it's being held back, maybe because of what the Kels did, maybe because you are finally using my potion*, Gwen said, and patted Lance's knee.

What do we need to do? I asked.

It's not clear, just be aware, the darkness is building, and I'm guessing by that, it's planning an attack. Gwen looked at Lance, then added, *You're carrying my ring?*

He pulled it out of his pocket to show her, and she looked mildly relieved. *Good, keep it close. I was going to have it turned into something you could wear, but... it never felt right to alter it. That's why it's still the same form as when your grandfather gave it to me, minus your brothers' stones, that is. Put it on a necklace, wear it around your neck. I can feel that you will need it.*

Lance nodded, and I could tell Gwen was preparing to leave. *Grandma,* Lance said, catching her attention. *Do you forgive us for avoiding coming back here? For never visiting you? I can understand if you don't...*

She put her hand on his knee and smiled. *There isn't anything to forgive, I missed you and your brothers, but I knew you needed the time, all of you did. It's working out now anyway, just like it was meant to.*

She stood and kissed his temple, like she'd done to me more times than I could remember. *Forgive yourself, Lance. You did the best you could, given the circumstances.*

He nodded, and again, I felt more layers of his pain begin to heal.

Gwen looked over at me and smiled, then slowly disappeared.

That night, I held Lance as silent tears flowed from him. My heart ached for him, as he processed all the betrayal and hurt mixed with the loss of someone who'd loved him unconditionally. I understood on a soul level how he was feeling, because I'd felt Gwen's loss just as deeply.

When Saturday morning came around, I was so warmly snuggled into Lance that I would've paid big money to avoid having to leave his side. Unlike him and Gwen, I'd never been a morning person. I preferred to sleep late and then stay up late into the night.

Years as Gwen's roommate had forced me to change my habits. Unfortunately, during the time since she'd passed, I'd slipped back into my same old sleep patterns, but now it seemed her grandson would be the one to ensure I got back to their routine.

Lance reached over and kissed my forehead. "I'm going for a quick run. I'm not even gonna ask you to join me," he said. "Although the cold rain on your face is exhilarating."

"Ugh," I moaned. "I'll have coffee made for your crazy ass when you get back. How's that?"

He kissed me on the lips, laughing and ignoring our morning breath, and said, "Deal."

I managed to crawl out of bed after he left and turned the coffee pot on. Since Lance had been back, I prepped my coffee at night before we went to bed, knowing I wouldn't have the energy to go through the process until I'd at least had my shower.

I was fresh out of the shower and fixing my first cup when Lance returned, soaking wet and fucking hot as a coal in the bottom of a fire pit.

"How can you be that sexy this early in the morning?" I asked for like the fifth time this week.

He just laughed and came over to me, pulling my dry, warm, showered body into his cold, wet one.

I squealed in a very unsexy way, but he just laughed, kissed me, and dashed back toward the bathroom.

When I felt the tell-tale signs of Gwen, my heart picked up a beat. It'd been a few days since she and Lance had talked, and I was eager to see her again.

You two are getting on well, I see, she said, smiling.

Yeah, you old matchmaker. Don't get too full of yourself, though.

She chuckled, but her usual mirth was subdued. *Gwen, what's going on?* I asked.

You should be prepared. I'm not sure what level of danger you're in, but even since the last time we spoke, I can feel that the cantation has gotten stronger. I have to assume it means to attack and soon.

I sighed. *Well, it's been nice while it lasted. Since Lance did a protection spell to banish his father, it's been quiet here.*

She looked surprised. *You got Lance to do spells?*

I nodded. *Didn't even have to push very hard, he was willing.*

Damn, I was surprised that you got him to use his third eye to see me, but to use spells? You're better than I thought, she said, and this time her smile was bright.

Were you there when Katan began recruiting him to be mayor?

Gwen leaned back and laughed. *No, but I should've seen it myself. He'd be perfect.*

I think so too. But I think it scares him a bit.

You'll be surprised at how little fear he has for that kind of role. It's not like he hasn't been a leader for years.

Just not in a small town on the coast of Oregon, full of and run by witches, I said.

He'd love it, was made for it, Gwen said, sounding proud.

She looked over my shoulder, and her smile waned. *Damn, I wish I knew how to beat that son of a bitch back.*

I couldn't hold it back and let the laughter roll. She looked at me funny until I was able to get myself under control.

What? she asked.

Gwen, honey, that cantation is your son, or at least an ugly aspect of him. If it's a son of a bitch...

Her eyes grew big and had she still been in human form, I know she'd have hit my arm. *Oh, my gods... you're right. And damn it, I am a bitch and don't mind anyone knowing it,* she said, sending me into another fit of laughter.

Lance walked in as I was laughing, and he cocked an eyebrow. When I explained what'd happened, he burst out laughing too. "Grandma, you aren't a bitch, at least not much of one. That time you squirted me and Kyle with the water hose for stepping on your daffodils, that might've—"

He stopped midsentence when Gwen went over to him and pinched his upper arm. "Did she just pinch me?" he asked, and I laughed again.

"She said you had it coming, and would do it again now if she could."

"Love you too, Grandma!" he said, chuckling and rubbing the spot.

We sat down in the living room, and I helped him use his third eye again, so he could see us all. Gwen repeated her concerns that she'd just told me a moment ago

What should we do? he asked.

Gwen sat silently, shaking her head. *I don't know if there's anything you can do other than wait it out. Wear the ring I gave you. Oh, and drink more of my potion. In fact, you should both cover yourselves in it too.*

When she mentioned that to him, Lance cringed. *Smell like my grandmother? No offense, Grandma, but that doesn't sound appealing.*

She laughed so hard, she blinked in and out of focus a few times.

Knowing the ring didn't fit him, I jumped up and went to my bedroom, found a white gold chain I hadn't used in years, and came back, handing it to Lance. "Here, you can put the ring on that and wear it around your neck," I said aloud, seeing as Gwen had vanished once again.

He regarded it for a moment, then complied. "Is it gold?" he asked, and I nodded. "Isn't this worth quite a bit?"

"Yeah, but your safety is worth more. Don't worry about it. If you don't end up needing it, you can give it back, not that I need it. I've not used that necklace since the late nineties."

Both of us snickered, and I assumed he remembered how gold chains were in fashion back then.

Having the ring attached to something Lance was wearing seemed to mollify Gwen, at least enough for her to let us go get set up for the Harvest Moon Festival without her feeling like she needed to remain with us on guard.

She'd never said, but I had a feeling being in corporal form, even when we were using our third eyes to communicate, took something from her. If I was right, and her concerns were founded, we needed her to be in top form, so it was best she didn't use up too much of her energy. That was especially true in the event Lance needed her again, and soon.

TWENTY

LANCE

I FOLLOWED DREW AND the rest of the Guild down to the beach below his home. I watched in astonishment as the group lifted their hands into the air and the fog and mist parted, not unlike a curtain, until the sun began to shine through into the magically made circle.

The circle then began to surround the entire town, and it was just a little creepy how the clouds surrounded us. "The ability to control the weather," I said, shaking my head.

Drew came over and kissed my cheek as he and the others walked past. "Hey," I asked, following after them, "How long will this last?"

"Provided we don't get any storms, and the weather remains as passive as it is now, the spell should last through the night, but if more aggressive weather batters it, it may only last until noon."

"Are you expecting bad weather?" I asked.

Drew smiled. "Nope, just the same mist we have now."

"Cool," I said, and heard the older people around us chuckling.

Considering the advanced age of most of the Air Guildmembers, walking long distances wasn't really an option, so they piled into their vehicles and drove down to the Grange House. Drew and I decided to walk and enjoy the now beautiful sunny weather.

He slipped his hand into mine, and we walked like that through the town. People waved cheerfully as they saw us. I was old enough to have experienced all the hatred thrown at gay couples through the years, and even when I was married to Tom, he and I never were much for PDA, but this felt so right. Accepted wasn't even the right word. It was more like welcomed. That was when it became more apparent that welcoming had always been what this community was for me.

When I'd visited here as a child with my brothers, then briefly lived here, the community had welcomed me. Why had it taken so damned long for me to realize that? So many years I could've been with people who actually gave a damn about me.

It wasn't like I wasn't supported in my life. I had my brothers, my daughter, Jennie, and always had friends. Jennie's parents, her dad in particular, had always been one of my best friends. When he transitioned, that just brought us closer. Gerald, even though the man was a politician and would be until he left this life, had always been there for me too, but I'd forgotten what it felt like for an entire community to embrace and care about me. Suddenly, I wanted that in my life again. As we entered the clearing that led to the Grange House, I realized my entire life had been changing, making way for this.

I saw Katan from a distance, and he looked up and smiled. *Damn, the man already knew*... and now I had to acknowledge that I was very likely going to accept the position. I didn't even feel upset, anxious, or disturbed that I'd be taking on such a leadership position. The truth was it felt right the first time Katan mentioned it. Mayor Lance Franklyn. *What the fuck?*

By the time I got to the group of Guild members, Katan was smiling. He didn't say anything though, just clapped me on the back and got back to work helping get the place set up for the day's festivities.

"Sperm Daddy?" I heard from behind me.

I shook my head as I turned around. "I told you not to call me that, girl!" I said as I swooped Jennie up into my arms.

She shrugged me off like she always did. "I'm glad you're here. I meant to come by your house in Salem, but we've been so busy."

A group of people came up behind Jennie then. One of them was my brother Crea, and he was holding hands with the handsome Eli Bane. I pulled Crea into a hug when he got to me.

"How the hell did you bag a hottie like this one?" I asked, and both my brother and Eli blushed.

"Gods, you're an idiot, Lance," he said, shaking his head. "This is my fiancé..." He let the word hang for several moments, the light dancing in his eyes "...Eli Bane, and Eli, this is my idiot older brother, Lance Franklyn."

"Idiot? I can still kick your ass, little brother," I said, laughing.

"'Cept now my big-muscled boyfriend will kick yours right back!" he said, and Eli was for real eyeing me like he could do just that.

"Well, lucky for you both, I'm not looking for kicking butts today, just for having some fun."

Crea playfully tapped my arm with his shoulder. I then had another moment of questioning why the hell I had kept myself at such a distance from my family. Just like Chemeketa, Crea was one of my people, someone I really cared a lot about. I was coming to realize I'd hurt more than just myself by keeping everyone at arm's length all these years.

"Sperm Daddy, I want you to meet my girlfriend, Scarlett," Jennie said, causing me to groan inwardly, but before I could chastise her, she quickly continued, "Scarlett, this is my Sperm Daddy, Lance."

"You can just call me Dad or Lance. You can leave the sperm out of it."

"Not likely. No sperm would mean no me," she said, and I blushed as she chuckled.

"Anyway—" I said deliberately, "—it's a pleasure to meet you, Scarlett."

The name absolutely fit the short, redheaded pixie of a woman who stood before me. "The pleasure's mine. Oh," she said when Drew walked over and ducked under my arm. "Hey, Drew. Do you have anything you need help with?"

Drew smiled at her. "No, but your dad can help us. Is he on his way?"

Scarlett nodded. "Yes, but he had Kel business this morning. Drew, have you met Jennie?" she asked.

"No, actually, we always seemed to miss one another when she came to visit Gwen," he said, and took her hand. "Jennie, I've heard lovely things about you."

Jennie had been staring at us since Drew slipped under my arm. "Are you dating?" she asked us.

I looked at Drew and back at her. "Yeah, sorta. We've not named what we're doing though."

Drew winked at me, then looked at my brother. "Crea, it's great to see you again, and Eli, I hear you're taking on the job of keeping the woodland creatures happy."

"Forester, but sure, that's part of it," Eli said, and shook Drew's hand.

"Well, why don't you all come into the Grange House, and we'll have coffee and some of the homemade scones Jack Henry made. I'm keen to get at least one before they're gone," Drew said, and winked at us. "Jack's baked goods are legendary around these parts."

There was little danger of running out of scones. There were piles of them sitting on the tables under huge covers, not unlike what you'd expect to see at a high-end brunch.

I picked up one of the scones, bit into it and had a mouth orgasm right there in front of everyone. "My god, these are... what the hell does he do to make them this good?" I asked, causing Drew to chuckle.

"Magic," he said, then led the group over to sit next to the big fireplace, burning delightfully in the corner of the building.

We sat together, each of us taking turns talking. Crea, Eli, and Jennie told me about their trip to Toronto. Of course, Jennie was more than excited about the commission since she'd be helping Eli with it. I wanted to ask her a million questions about Scarlett and working for Eli, but it wasn't the place, so instead, I turned to my brother.

"So, you're taking a job here in Chemeketa?" I asked.

He nodded and smiled. "Yes, the field on the back side of the Grange House has been a cow pasture for years. The community is turning it into a garden to supply fresh produce, especially for the folks moving into the new senior housing that's going up across the street."

"It's what you were born to do, brother," I said, remembering all the plants Crea used to grow at our parents' house. Both the inside and outside of our home were filled with flowers and plants from the time Crea was old enough to know how to plant them.

"And you, Eli, you're moving here as well?" I asked.

He nodded. "You should come up to the cabin, we're having it remodeled."

"And you're living there while you are?" I asked, thinking how little patience my obsessive brother had with chaos.

Seeing my expression, Crea chuckled. "No, I'm renting a room from Mr. Henry." He cuddled into Eli, smiling. "Our introduction to romance was a bit rocky." He looked sad for a few moments, then said, "We had to deal with Dad."

The group fell silent as if they were all holding their breath. "Anyway..." Crea said after the pregnant pause, "...things have happened so fast, we've decided to live apart until the cabin is done. That way, we can grow into our relationship."

"That and you don't have to be in the middle of a construction zone?" I eyed my brother, who laughed.

"You don't forget anything, Lance. I was just a teenager, and they were tearing up my gardens."

"They were adding on a room for Kyle to live in."

"I wasn't prepared to lose my azaleas."

I explained to the group how twelve-year-old Crea had blown a gasket when his prized plants were dug up by the bulldozers when they added a room and bathroom onto our home for our younger brother to have his own space. Or, more accurately, so Crea could have his.

That reminded me of the good times with our family. Our parents... had cared. Okay, our father had cared. They had fucked it all up in the end, but at least at one time they'd cared about us enough to build an extra room for a young man who needed his privacy.

I shook it off as Donna Rummel came into the room to get Crea, Eli, and Jennie. "I need all the Earth Guild folks to come help dry the ground, so we don't end up turning the place into a swamp out there today."

Jennie winked at me as she walked by, answering my question about her going with them. As I let myself think about it, I guessed Jennie and Crea were more alike than her and me. She'd always loved everything related to the earth, so of course, as this crazy, sweet little town got into all our souls, she would prove to be most attracted to the Earth Guild.

When they had all gone, Drew leaned over and kissed me. "You okay?" he asked.

"Oh, life is coming at me fast, but it's good. Everything feels right."

He smiled then and captured my lips again. "Jennie seems happy. Gwen adored her. You know she was here a lot the past few years, although I always seemed to miss her. It's my understanding that's how she and Scarlett met. If you ask me, I'd be willing to guess there's a wedding in your near future."

We both froze. I swallowed hard to get the shock of the fact that the wedding might very well be my own. I mean, I swore to all that was holy I'd never marry again, not after Tom, but I could, even in the short time I'd known him, see myself being married to Drew.

"So, *Jennie*—" I said, emphasizing her name. "—will be a beautiful bride."

Drew visibly relaxed and grabbed my hand. "Yes, she will, now come on, we have work to do."

Twenty-One

Drew

S EEING LANCE'S FAMILY SO happy together must've momentarily short-circuited my brain. One minute I was talking about Lance's daughter, the next, I accidentally insinuated our relationship was much more than it was.

I was glad he quickly let me off the hook, but I watched, assuming the poor man would go running for the hills any moment. I didn't know what had got into me really. Sure, Gwen had been like family, and I missed that sense of companionship, but I'd never thought about marriage. I didn't think it'd ever make sense for me or my lifestyle, what with traveling for weeks on end touring with my band.

I was less a sworn bachelor than a proactive avoider of all things conforming. Handfasting, maybe, but a traditional marriage? Not in this lifetime, but then, why didn't the thought of it with Lance scare me?

I wanted to blame Gwen, but I knew when she wasn't meddling any longer, and although I could feel her close by, she was preoccupied with the undercurrent of darkness that still threatened us. The truth was, this wasn't

Gwen's doing. It was just me finally meeting someone who made my insides go all weird and wonky. Was that what being in love felt like? I wouldn't know.

As the day wore on, Lance helped the kids and adults with their kites, laughing like a kid himself when one of us sent a breeze to lift the kites up into the sky, and I fell even more for him, not that I wasn't already pretty smitten.

We'd spent over a week together, and the man touched my soul in and out of bed. He had Gwen's sense of humor, although definitely darker. He was also a bit of a prankster, which, to be honest, I sort of loved.

I could so easily see myself growing old with someone like Lance. And I assumed that was why I felt the darkness battering against my, Gwen's, and Lance's defenses so hard.

The day drew to a close as it always did with the evening potluck. Like many small communities, Chemeketa boasted some naturally talented cooks, especially among the Earth Guild and hedge witches. Plenty of others tried to cook and, well, just couldn't, but that didn't stop them from contributing to every community potluck.

After all the years I'd lived here, I knew which foods to avoid. *Not that I needed magical abilities for that,* I thought, chuckling to myself. Just looking at which dishes were going the fastest and which ones hadn't been touched at all was clue enough.

With our plates piled high, I sat leaned up against Lance as his family surrounded us. Alegia and Frank had joined us as well, mostly because I doubted Scarlett was going to let Jennie out of her sight. The electric love between those two was palpable.

The Fire Guild, all six of its members, was preparing to throw up fireworks using their fire energy to cap the day's festivities. There was always a concern that once the Guild's fireworks were let loose, the weather would rush back in. This was due to the fire sources having to pull their energy from farther away, considering the fires in the earth in this part of the world had long been dormant.

To do that, we had to lower the magical shields, especially with so few fire elementals and all but one being over sixty now.

The mayor stood and announced it was time for fireworks, which was the signal for me and the other three Guild leaders to stand and send energy to one another to let down the shields.

The first surge of energy came immediately after the shields fell and burst into a beautiful dragon that swept through the sky, then dashed down toward the crowd, causing everyone to scream and laugh.

It was then I glanced at Lance. His face was pale, and his eyes big. He looked like he was about to pass out. I immediately reached for him, and the moment we touched, my body was thrust onto the ground next to his. The next thing I knew, we were both floating high in the air above our bodies.

"Fuck," I said. "This ain't good!"

TWENTY-TWO

LANCE

THE NIGHT WAS GOING so well. I mean, I was with my brother, his fiancé, my daughter, and my... *boyfriend? Lover?* My relationship with Drew was hard to define. Jennie had questioned if we were dating, which was probably the best description of us right now.

The day had been perfect—laughter, games, cute kids with kites, and ice cream, and everything you could imagine at an end-of-the-season community festival. It brought back so many happy memories of when we'd come to Chemeketa as kids with our dad, and spent the night with our grandparents just having fun.

The shift from contentment to fear happened instantly. The moment the Guild leaders stood and cast a light rope to connect them, the world began to feel dark. It was almost as if I'd been hit with a fever, not unlike when I'd been so hideously sick not so long ago.

I broke out in a sweat, but at the same time, I was impossibly cold. I was just about to retch onto the ground when Drew looked over and saw me. He reached out and put his hand on me, and instantly, we were thrust out of our bodies and into the skies above the crowd.

"This ain't good!" Drew yelled, and when I looked to my right, the darkness had already begun to sweep from the edges of the forest toward us.

"Get behind me, Lance," Drew said, and even though he wasn't in corporeal form, he tried to push me behind him. Of course, his hand, like smoke, just passed through me.

"No, Drew, this isn't your fight. This is between him and me," I said, knowing it was my father once again.

As the fog leveled up to us, I yelled at it. "I'm not afraid of you, and it's time for this shit to stop once and for all!"

Malevolent laugher drifted through the fog, before a voice just as nasty, said, "And who is going to stop me? *You?* You are weak, you are worthless. How can a faggot, a nasty queer, stop the power that flows through me?"

My grandmother appeared by my side then, and answered the question, "You aren't powerful. You are not even whole. Love is what will conquer you. Love I have for my grandson, love I have for my friend, even love I have for you, at least the part of you that's still human."

The fog laughed again and then began taunting my grandmother. "The love you have for me? You never loved me, woman. You loved your power, and you coming here to this place of dark magic, that's what made me. You are why I exist."

Grandma laughed. "Your lies are pathetic, creature. We are what you fear the most, because my family and this community represent all that's light, all that's good. Be gone with you!"

She thrust out her arms, and with it came light the color of rich earth. The fog separated where the power struck, and the entity laughed. Within seconds it formed what appeared to be a humanoid. Its hand held a sharp dagger made of what looked like obsidian.

"I will end this now!" the creature bellowed and rushed forward with the dagger, stabbing at the cords that tethered Drew and me to our bodies. In the back of my mind, I remembered hearing a warning that if a cord was severed while having an out-of-body experience, the person would die. I could feel myself starting to panic and glanced over at Drew, who was pulling power into himself.

When he released it, a great wind began to blow toward the shadows, forcing them back. Out of the corner of my eye, I saw the wind had blown the dragon fireworks away, and now the entire community was looking up at us. Alegia, Donna, and even Crea and Eli stood over our motionless bodies, I could see whisps of energy flowing into us, and for a brief moment, gratitude engulfed me as I let their love and self-sacrifice fill me.

I only had seconds to notice what was happening on the ground, because the entity gathered its strength again, and as Drew's wind subsided, it drove itself toward Drew's cord.

The diamond ring hanging around my neck began to glow, and even in spirit form, I could feel it lifting up and away from me. I knew in that instant, while Drew's life hung in the balance, that my grandma's ring was the key.

I reached for it, and when my hand clasped the ring, it shifted into a sword. Not a real sword, but one made of air that I could actually feel. The sword was white and looked like clouds reflecting the light. My hand gripped the pommel, and I swung the sword at the entity, causing it to dash away before the dagger it held could sever Drew's cord.

I began swinging wildly, determined to save Drew and myself. That's when my grandmother's hand rested on my shoulder. "Be calm, Lance," she said. "You have the power to end this, but not by yourself. Trust Drew to help you send your father's cantation away."

I stopped swinging. Drew released another gale, which forced the fog back once again. When my eyes met Drew's, he smiled. "Ready to get rid of this thing?" he asked.

My heart sang more than ever before, and seeing the determined look on Drew's face banished my fear and created a resolve I never knew I could possess against my father.

Just as the cantation rushed toward us, Drew put his hand over mine and together we lifted the sword and brought it down upon the darkness before it could render the lethal blow.

There was a screech like nothing I'd ever heard before peeling out of the dark fog as the sword pierced it, like some wild, otherworldly beast in its death throes.

The moment the screeching started, the sword burst into a brilliant light, driving the darkness far away from us and the town.

As I stared at Drew, the light drew back upon us, and a white diamond-shaped tattoo formed in the middle of his forehead.

He reached up and touched my forehead, a look of awe on his beautiful face.

"Matching tattoos?" I asked, and he grinned.

I looked back then and saw my grandmother hovering in front of us. "You've done it," she said, smiling. "You've driven it back. Go now, my loves, and enjoy your lives together and know I will always love you both with everything I am."

As we embraced, kissing one another, I heard the entire town cheering below us and felt something warm forming on my left ring finger.

I woke next to Drew as our spirits slipped back into our bodies. My finger still felt warm, and when I looked at it, I saw I was wearing a white-gold band. Drew pulled himself up from the ground and my eyes followed as he glanced at his hand as well, only to see an identical band on his left ring finger.

"I think my grandmother's giving us a hint."

Drew blushed. "Maybe a bit more than that," Katan said from a distance as he came toward us. "Your grandmother was, in fact, a justice of the peace before she passed."

Drew and I looked at one another and burst out laughing. "It'd be just like her meddling self to conduct a wedding ceremony from the other side," Alegia said, trying to sneer, but a smile still managed to filter through.

I felt a flood of emotions and couldn't resist kissing Drew on the mouth. "I do," I whispered under my breath just for him to hear.

"Careful, I could easily take this as a real proposal," he whispered back as he nuzzled my neck. So much for my not reveling in PDAs.

I pulled back and winked at him but didn't say anything else. When we were alone, and not surrounded by an entire town of people, I'd get him naked and propose to him like a man you loved with your entire soul should be proposed to... when he was too overcome by our lovemaking to say no.

Twenty-Three

Drew

FRANK KNOCKED ON MY door the Thursday before Lance had to go back to Salam for work. When I came out, I saw him standing with a group of men I'd never met before, but knew instinctively were all Kels.

"Morning, Frank," I said, confused.

"Good morning. Can we speak to the mayor?" he asked.

"Um, Katan isn't here, Frank."

He chuckled. "I meant the upcoming mayor."

I cocked an eyebrow at my neighbor but nodded. "Lance, you have company," I hollered into the house. "Would you like to come in?" I asked the group.

Lance stood and greeted everyone as they all came in and sat in the living room.

"Mayor," one of the men said to Lance. "I'm Edward Edenfield, leader of the Kels who occupy the forest. These are my council brothers." He then proceeded to introduce them all to us.

With the introductions made, Lance smiled. "Nice to meet you all, but you know I'm not the mayor."

Edward shook his head and said, "You are or will be, and we need to speak to the one who will be leading the town in the future."

I saw the resignation in Lance's face, and had I not known the Kels to be a serious people, I probably would've chuckled.

"How can I help you, gentlemen?" he asked.

"We've come to discuss the Kels' involvement with the town council."

I stood to go when Frank stopped me. "No, Drew, don't go. This involves you too."

I sat back down, concerned at the Kel leaders arriving in such an ominous way.

Edward looked back at Lance. "Our seers have witnessed much in their visions, things that involve undoing the foundations our ancestors set in place long ago. Magical beings are being displaced, volcanos, long ago tamed, are threatening to erupt. Not to mention the climate changes that are occurring because of human greed. The Kels understand we can no longer hide in our villages within the great woods." Edward looked hesitantly toward the other men, who all nodded in unison.

He took a deep breath and let it out slowly before saying, "We believe we must join forces with the other Guilds in Chemeketa, for it is going to take the entire town to reestablish the boundaries of power if the world is to survive what's coming."

I immediately thought of the curse Lance's father had cast upon his three sons, when one of the elders in the group turned to me. "I'm a seer," he said. "You are concerned about the curse you and your man have just overcome. Although all the dark energies are becoming stronger and thus tipping the balance from light to dark, he is not the only reason we are here."

That eased my mind, if only slightly, and Edward nodded. "We felt the dark energy when my brother, Eli Bane, brought his man Crea into the forest. We helped banish it then, and again when Frank called us to banish it from you and the mayor. We sense that dark energy has not yet been vanquished, but this is bigger than it."

He turned back to Lance. "We offer our involvement to the town of Chemeketa. Mayor, I know you are new to this area, as is your brother Crea, but you should know, the Kel people have always stayed apart from the rest of the town. We've done that on purpose to preserve our culture and to keep our form of energy pure. So, you should know it's significant for us to make this commitment after all this time."

He turned to me then, and said, "We will also become active participants in the Air Guild."

I nodded, fully recognizing the significance of what was happening. "Are you willing to lead the Air Guild?" I asked Edward, and his face instantly showed surprise.

"You would be willing to step down to let the Kel lead it?" he asked.

I chuckled. "It's not my place to lead the Guild, Mr. Edenfield. I've only agreed to do so temporarily until a permanent replacement can be found. Since you're already the chosen leader of the Kels, and since your people are all air energy, it only makes sense that you run the Air Guild."

"You don't think the other members of the Guild will object?" he asked, still sounding shocked.

"They will need to vote, of course, but you know the Air Guild in Chemeketa has never been strong. Most have always believed that was because the air energies are so strong among the Kels. Given you are all willing to step up and join the Guild, I don't believe any of our current members will object."

I didn't add that they were all ancient and concerned that the younger generation hadn't come back to Chemeketa to take over from them.

"Then, in that case, I would be willing to lead the Guild."

I explained that would entail holding Guild meetings and attending the town council once a week, as well as helping during events and festivals. He nodded as I spoke.

"So, where shall we meet? It's my understanding many of the Kels have pledged never to leave the forest. I'm sure most of the Guild are too old to trek into the forest on their own."

Edward smiled. "I think I may have a solution. My brother, Eli, has just moved into the forest. His home is large enough to gather all the Kel people. It's also an auspicious place, sitting atop an extinct volcano and looking out over the entire forest and much of Chemeketa. If he's willing to allow us to meet there, would you agree to that?"

Lance chuckled. "I'm sure Crea would love it. My brother has always loved to entertain."

Edward winked at Lance. "I'll speak to Eli and let you know."

They left, and I sat down on the sofa next to Lance. "So, Mayor Franklyn, you're already making changes."

"No, I... ugh ...I should probably speak to Katan."

"Yep," I said, and laughed as he pulled out his phone and asked me for his number.

While Lance spoke to Katan, I went into the garden, opened my third eye, and called to Gwen.

She took a moment to show up, but when she did, I told her what had happened. *Do you think I should convene the council, so they can scry these concerns?* I asked.

Gwen looked disappointed. *I'm not allowed to advise you on those aspects of the living, Drew. My connection with this side is tenuous at best, but I can say there is indeed an imbalance between the dark and the light. One should never ignore an imbalance, as it almost always leads to change, and those changes must be prepared for.*

Like with the cantation. That's why he was so powerful? The balance of energy from light to dark enhanced him, didn't it? I asked.

She nodded. *I believe so, yes, but now you will see things change in even more significant ways.*

Thanks, Gwen, and I will respect the boundaries. I know you have another grandchild to save from his father.

She smiled. *I'm not gone yet, Drew, but yes, my focus must be to protect my grandchildren. When they have overcome their father's curse, then I may rest.*

She looked tired then, and suddenly I was sad she was stuck here like this. No living person knew what was on the other side, but spirits trapped on this side of the veil often suffered as a result. As an air sign, I'd always had some connection with those who'd transitioned, but hadn't passed through, none as clear and accessible as

Gwen, but enough to know it wasn't peaceful for them to remain here among the living.

I returned to the living room as Lance finished his conversation with Katan. When he'd hung up, I said, "Tomorrow night is our council meeting. I'd like you to attend, as I'm going to ask the council to scry the visions the Kels mentioned their seers having. As the new mayor, you'll want to be aware of them yourself."

"I guess everyone's come to terms with my being mayor but me," he said mournfully.

"Chemeketa is an odd little town, and because we all have some connection with the universe, we tend to know what we want. You're who we want. Besides, you're going to make an amazing mayor."

He kissed me and sighed against my lips. "I guess, but I still feel a bit overwhelmed by how fast it's happening."

"No problem, I'll help you settle in," I said, and slipped my hand down between his legs.

"Oh, I like your help," he said, and we collapsed on the sofa with me on top of him.

TWENTY-FOUR

LANCE

THE SCRYING WAS...WELL, weird. Images swam around us, and I saw what looked to be dragons, followed by a volcano erupting. Seals swam in the ocean, chased by large sea monsters. There was also a lot of chanting, and ghostly entities floating in the air that I recognized from the night I'd dreamed of Drew. Of course, I could now piece together those were the Kels I'd seen.

Ultimately, when the visions cleared, the council looked grave. "Changes are coming, and we must prepare," Katan said. "Lance, I know you're finishing up your duties in Salem, but know your leadership will be needed more than ever."

He looked at the group and sighed. "My time on this earth is coming to an end. In the visions, I saw two, maybe three years before my time is over. That will only give me a short time to work with you, Lance. And I believe you will need all the help you can get."

Donna placed her hand on Katan's shoulder. I hadn't seen anything that showed me Katan's time was limited, but obviously the others had.

"I'll let my office know I'm transitioning to this position, but shouldn't there be an election?" I asked.

Katan nodded. "For those in the council who believe Lance should become the next mayor of Chemeketa, please raise your hand."

The entire group did, including Drew.

"Wait, that's it?" I asked.

Donna chuckled. "No, there will be a formal election involving all of the town's residents, but that vote will be to confirm the council's choice of mayor. I seriously doubt with your experience, it will be anything but a landslide victory."

I sighed. "Okay, well, I'll inform my office and make arrangements so that when I'm not absolutely needed in Salem, I can be here."

"And he'll be staying with me," Drew said, earning a series of knowing smirks from the group.

"As it should be," Donna said and stood. "I'm sorry all, but scrying wears me out. I'm going home. Katan, you might want to conclude the meeting."

He smiled, but there was sadness laced in it. Seeing your own end couldn't be easy, even when you were old enough to know it was coming. "The meeting is adjourned," Katan said, without following Robert's Rules of Order, something the others noticed as well. However, no one objected, and we all got up to leave.

Katan pulled me aside as I began helping put the chairs away. "I know Drew said you'll be staying with him, but I'd like you to consider spending a week or two with my wife and me. I have a lot to show you, and much of that can happen through a spiritual connection as we both sleep."

I looked perplexed, and he smiled again. "We have many ways of doing things that aren't available to the general public, but with the visions of tonight, Lance, I don't know how much more time I have left. Unlike sweet Gwen, when it's time for me to go, I would rather cross the veil and be done with it. So, I think we should fast-forward the learning process if at all possible."

I nodded and felt the sadness within him. "I'd be honored to stay with you and your wife, Katan."

He patted my arm then and said goodnight.

As we rode home together, I told Drew what Katan had told me. "Yes, I think he's probably right," Drew confirmed. "You should acquire the understanding you need as fast as possible, then the rest of us can guide you if Katan passes before your education is complete."

"Wow, this is all so strange, right?" I asked.

"Yes, when you're new, but trust me, it'll all feel natural after you begin to receive instruction. For now, just roll with it. Besides, like Donna, scrying wears me out. I'm gonna go brush my teeth and go to sleep. Why don't you join me?"

When I wagged my eyebrows, he chuckled. "Maybe tomorrow, unless you wanna be screwing while I sleep."

"I can wait. Why am I not tired?" I asked as we went into the house.

Drew shrugged as he walked toward the bathroom. "Scrying is probably something you're good at. That's something you can work on with Alegia if you're interested. I'm sure she'd love to teach our new mayor all about that skill."

He disappeared into the bathroom, and I couldn't help but wonder if maybe he was right. I had a lot of catching up to do, and a lot to learn about my capabilities. And for the first time, I was excited about the possibilities.

TWENTY-FIVE

DREW

WEEKS PASSED QUICKLY WITH all the gigs my band had booked. We ended up doing a Christmas tour in Europe, filling in for a band who'd backed out at the last minute. It was fun, but I missed Lance way too much.

I'd decided a while ago not to pursue fame and fortune, and now that Lance was a part of my life, I knew I'd made the right choice. Success for me was waking up next to my man and occasionally blocking the fog so the town could enjoy a sunny day or dry community festival.

Speaking of festivals, I'd be getting home just in time for the winter solstice. I wanted to be home to celebrate it with Lance. He was just beginning to grasp all the nuances of the craft and was already incredibly powerful, more so than any other air energy in Chemeketa, including the Kels, which was saying something, considering their powers and energy were magnified by their ancestors.

The moment we touched down, I was ready to sprint off the plane to get home. Lance had agreed to pick us up at the airport and deliver us back to Chemeketa.

The moment I came out of the security area, I saw Lance, and couldn't help but launch myself into his arms. Of course, it was to the laughter of my bandmates.

"Gods, I missed you," I said as I kissed him thoroughly before pulling back.

"You can't have missed me more than I missed you," he said, and Lily came up behind us and made some snarky comment about getting a room.

"Jealous much?" I tossed back.

We were as exhausted as ever when coming off a tour, but we were still in good spirits, and the band teased Lance unmercifully as he drove us back to Chemeketa.

As soon as it was just him and me, I attacked him, stripping him as we went until we were back in the bedroom. Finally, I could do all the things to his body I'd been thinking about for the past few weeks.

As we both fell back on the bed, spent and lying in our post-sex bliss, I rolled over, snuggled in, and kissed him deeply. "I'm so tired, but I plan to do that a lot more, starting in the morning."

He chuckled and wrapped his arms around me. "There'll be plenty of time, love, plenty of time."

Twenty-Six

Lance

I'VE NEVER BEEN EMBARRASSED by my body. I worked out, ate right, and jogged every day if I could, so I was in fairly good shape, but I wasn't all that comfortable being naked amid a group of people, even if it was to *enhance a spell*, whatever that meant.

Grandma's coven, who'd all decided they needed to use Drew's house to bring in the new year, said it was okay if I wore a robe, as long as it was made from all-natural fibers.

That was how I found myself outside in my robe on a cold December night, the day after the solstice—because, according to Drew, the new year began when the days began to lengthen again, not January first—among a group of naked old people chanting away in my late grandmother's garden.

I was pleased they had at least warmed the circle, as they called the area where they were performing their magic, because the flimsy robe did very little to keep the cold at bay.

Just as the chanting began to subside, a large flash of lightning stretched across the sky, accompanied by the smell of ozone.

Several of the women gasped, but it was quickly replaced by chuckles as I looked at the ground in the middle of the circle, and saw my little brother Kyle lying stark naked in front of us.

"Kyle? Hey, Kyle, wake up!" I said, and rushed toward him, afraid he was hurt. My brain should've been asking how he'd just appeared out of thin air. Clearly, I'd been in Chemeketa too long if this was beginning to feel normal.

"Lance?" he asked as he began to stir.

"Kyle, wake up!" I demanded again.

"What the fuck? What happened?" he asked.

Several chuckles came from behind me again. "Lance?" he asked, startled. "Did you summon me by magic?"

I shook my head and laughed. "You know I wouldn't have a clue how to do that. You were the one Grandma taught all that magic stuff to. Um, dude, you're kinda naked. Why don't you go with Drew to get some clothes? You're about his size. We can discuss the way you got here when you stop giving these folks a peep show."

"Shit, yeah," he said when he looked down at his naked form, and tried in vain to cover himself.

Donna stopped us before he could break the circle. "Kyle, you don't look injured, and we have a few more things to do before the evening is finalized. Besides, the only person here who isn't naked is your modest brother, you'll be fine."

"It's always a bad idea to break a circle, not to mention one on an auspicious night like tonight," one of the few men in the circle said. I couldn't remember the old guy's name, which I really was going to have to work on, considering this probably wouldn't be my last time standing nearly naked in a salt circle with him or the others.

Kyle stood there stoically, though he was blushing, as the coven said a few more chants and danced around the circle. They moved together quite beautifully and gracefully, which was all the more impressive when you considered most were well over sixty, before they closed the ceremony, got dressed, and left.

"We usually have a feast to celebrate, but I can see you need to tend to your brother," Donna said. "We'll convene down at the Grange House." She kissed my cheek then and paused. "You know it's his turn now, right?"

At first, I didn't understand what she meant, but then I realized she was talking about Dad and the cantation. "Damn, well, I guess that's why he popped up out of nowhere."

"That boy has always been the most stubborn of the three of you, although that's saying something. I'm guessing your poor grandmother had no choice but to zap him here, considering he was probably off chasing a volcano. The boy's been obsessed with them since I first met him," she said, shaking her head. Her fond smile turned sad then, which unsettled me.

"Anyway, take care, and tell him about your and Crea's experience. He needs to be prepared, and if I'm gonna guess, since he's a fire energy and loves volcanos, this one is going to be... explosive," she said before leaving.

I went in the house to find Kyle wearing Drew's clothes, and holding a steaming cup of something, and Drew sitting next to him, trying to comfort him.

"So, that happened," I said, and Kyle looked up. "Dang, brother, you look exhausted."

He nodded. "Yeah, I've done some shifting before, but only in a small circle, and never without a lot of prep. Grandma always said fire energy can do that sort of thing, but..."

"But, you weren't prepared for it," Drew said, looking concerned. "Do you know how it happened?" Kyle shook his head.

"I think Donna might've given me a clue. Both Crea and I have fended off Dad's nasty curse, so it's only logical it's now your turn. Being the last brother, I'm guessing it's going to be ugly."

Drew sighed. "I think you're right. Did you see your grandmother, by chance?" he asked.

"Yeah, why? And Dad's curse? Is that a real thing?" Kyle asked.

"How many men have you fallen in love with only to have it fall apart?" I asked.

Kyle shrugged and looked a bit shy. "I'm not really a commitment kind of guy. I'm too busy doing research, and a one-night stand is usually all the patience I have for a guy. I know that sounds bad..."

It was my turn to shrug. "Well, it probably saved you a lot of heartache, but I'm guessing that's about to change for you. Anyway—" I continued before Kyle could respond, "—let's get you to bed and tomorrow I'll call

Crea, and we'll fill you in on all the details. For now, you look like you're about to fall asleep."

He nodded as Drew smiled. "I just made the bed in your old room. I had a feeling I needed to, so it's all fresh and ready for you to tuck in."

Kyle smiled and hugged Drew, which, to be honest, made me a little jealous. I mean, Drew and Kyle were closer in age, and had gotten to know each other when Grandma was still alive, but when Drew made eye contact with me, the jealousy quickly passed. With just a look, I could see the love he held for me, and I hoped he could see the same reflected in my eyes.

As Kyle climbed the stairs to his old bedroom, I had a flashback to when we'd been kids and had just moved here. Kyle was the youngest and had been so young and vulnerable back then. In some ways, the blow-up with Dad had been worse for him, since he'd lost his family with fewer happy memories to cling to.

In other ways, I thought it helped him adjust better than Crea and me. Being older when Dad had cursed us definitely had its disadvantages, among them remembering those happy times that'd never come again.

Drew came over and pulled me into a hug. "I can tell you're concerned, but Kyle's strong and knows his gifts. Of the three of you, he'll be the most prepared for whatever your dad's cantation has in mind for him."

"I hope you're right," I said and snuggled into his arms. "Regardless, I'll give Crea a call tomorrow and maybe between you, me, him, and Eli, we can prepare Kyle for the worst of it. At least he won't have to go through all this alone."

"You were never alone, you both had Gwen. Sounds like she's got Kyle's back too."

"Yeah, about that, you better do your witchy thing and contact her. We'll need to know what she wants us to do. Maybe she can even be there tomorrow?"

Drew shrugged. "I'm guessing this isn't a journey we'll be taking with Kyle, but I'll see if she connects with me. I don't want to press too hard since her spirit seems tired, and having to spend too much time with us might prevent her from protecting Kyle."

I nodded. "Okay, sounds like a plan. But, for tonight, I'm thinking we need to celebrate the New Year, just you and me," I said as I slapped his ass, and sprinted to our bedroom.

Drew chuckled as he chased after me. "Oh, I fully agree!"

TWENTY-SEVEN

MEANWHILE...

THE FOG SWIRLED AROUND the outside of the nursing home window. The man began to stir for the first time since he'd had the stroke. The dark whispers had plagued him ever since, but in the past few weeks, they'd lost some of their strength.

As the beeps surrounding the bed began to sound, a voice echoed in the man's head. "Worry not, for we haven't lost all our powers yet. The next must face us between the light and the dark. We are even more powerful there," it said, and laughed wickedly.

NEXT...

When forced to choose between ending his father's curse and his fear of commitment, will Kyle embrace his destiny or will he turn away and let the world burn around him?

Continue the series with
Ruby Fire-Book Three of the Witch Brothers Saga

Available at your favorite bookseller

Join Blake's email list to get advance notice of new books and receive his occasional newsletter:

www.blakeallwood.com

MM Romance
By Blake Allwood

Transitions Series
Aiden Inspired
Suzie Empowered (MF Romance)
Bobby Transformed

Chance Series
Love By Chance
Another Chance With Love
Taking A Chance For Love

Romantic Series
Romantic Renovations (1)
Romantic Rescue (2)
Romantic Recon (3)

Melody Series
Melody of the Heart
Melody of the Snow

Road to Rocktoberfest Anthology
Changing His Tune - 2022

Coming Home Series (2023)
A Long Way Home
Family Home
Down Home
…and many more

Novellas
Tenacious
Moon's Place

Romantic Fantasy
By Adam J. Ridley

Big Bend Series
Love's Legacy (1)
Love's Heirloom (2)
Love's Bequest (3)

The Witch Brothers Series
Emerald Earth
Diamond Air
Ruby Fire
Sapphire Water

Blake Allwood was born in west Tennessee, then moved to Kansas City MO after earning a degree in Early Childhood Education from Graceland College in Lamoni, Iowa. He met his husband Shaun in 1995 and they officially married in 2015, once gay marriage was legalized; although they still consider Valentines Day 1995 as their true "anniversary date". Twenty-two years later (2017), after fostering 12 children together, he and his husband sold their home, purchased an RV and began traveling the country with their two dogs.

Typically, Blake can be found relaxing in the RV or by the fire with his laptop and their Jack Russell Terrier, Buddy, curled up between his legs demanding attention. Denver, their Siberian Husky mix is often asleep at his feet or playing tug of war with Blake's husband.

Most of Blake's stories are inspired by the places they have visited in their ongoing travels. His first book, *Aiden Inspired*, was released in 2019 and he has now written over 20 books. In 2023 he is releasing the *Coming Home* series which is comprised of ten-plus sweet contemporary romance novels that are based on a fictional town in his home state of Tennessee.

Blake also writes under the pen name of Adam J. Ridley for his urban fantasy fans looking for stories revolving around gay characters. His first series is The Witch Brothers Saga, starting with **Emerald Earth**.